EXTRACTION

DARK ROAD – BOOK FIVE

BRUNO MILLER

EXTRACTION:
Dark Road, Book Five

Copyright © 2018 Bruno Miller

Find out when Bruno's next book is coming out.
Join his mailing list for release news, sales, and the occasional survival tip. No spam ever.
http://brunomillerauthor.com/sign-up/

Published in the United States of America.

What would you do to survive?

Ben, Joel, Allie and their dog, Gunner, have faced down foes of all descriptions in their odyssey across the EMP ravaged country in search of their families.

Now as they approach the final leg of their journey the stakes are raised. With no way of knowing what danger lurks ahead, they encounter a new and never ending gauntlet of challenges and threats. Their ability to work as a team is tested anew, and they realize survival in this new world will require them all to make sacrifices.

Joel and Allie are forced to grow up fast in a world that offers little forgiveness for mistakes. Will the physical and mental demands be too much for them to handle? Will Ben's Army training and survival skills get them through and allow them to reunite with family?

Or will this be the last road they travel together?

THE DARK ROAD SERIES

For my readers —
thanks for taking this road trip with me.

- 1 -

Cloverdale, Indiana, was the next closest town on the map and their best chance to find the part they needed to fix the Blazer. Ben recalled seeing the sign a few miles back for the upcoming exit. The town itself was a few miles off the interstate.

That meant they had at least an eight-mile hike ahead of them unless they could find something before that. Ben was hoping for an auto parts store. The part they needed was a pretty common one and almost any automotive place should have it. He doubted old Chevy fuel pumps were high on the list of things people would loot.

The kids loaded water, food, and extra ammo into their backpacks along with the water filter and a few other items.

"Make sure everybody has a headlamp. We may be gone a while. It looks to be about eight miles or so to Cloverdale. That's probably our best bet to find the part we need." Ben checked his watch. It was already two in the afternoon, and he hated to admit it, but this was going to kill the rest of the day and some of the night. He added a few tools to his bag in case they came across a donor vehicle with a fuel pump.

Ben watched Gunner for a minute as the dog wandered around the woods near the kids. He was walking better now and putting more pressure on the leg that he'd injured during the confrontation with the wolf.

There was still a slight limp to his stride, but he was using it more than he had been this morning. Ben hoped the long hike ahead wouldn't be too hard on the dog.

"He's looking pretty good," Allie said.

Joel sighed. "I hope he's up for this."

Ben smiled. "He'll be fine. We'll keep an eye on him. If not, Joel can carry him."

Joel laughed. "Yeah, right."

Joel and Allie began unrolling the camo netting at the front of the truck and worked it back over the Blazer as they went.

"Make sure the doors are locked," Ben said.

"Everything is locked up except the back," Joel replied.

Ben still had the tailgate down and was adding a few things to his bag. Joel watched as he put one of the small gas stoves and a bottle of fuel in his bag, along with a small pot for boiling water.

"You think we'll be gone that long?" Joel asked.

"I hope not, but I don't want to get stuck out there without the means to cook a meal. After all that walking, we're going to need to eat." Ben pushed Gunner's collapsible bowl and a small Ziploc bag full of dog food across the tailgate toward Joel. "Do you have room for this?"

"I can fit it in mine," Allie offered. Gunner sniffed at the food as she stuffed it into her bag.

Ben slung the M24 over his shoulder and rooted around in the back of the Blazer for a minute before he closed it and locked the truck.

"Here you go, Allie." Ben handed her one of the knives he and Joel had salvaged from his store in Durango. "I should have given you one a long time ago. Try to keep it on you at all times."

"Thanks." Allie eyed the sleek, green-handled Spyderco G10 knife in her open palm. Gunner gave it a sniff but lost interest quickly when he realized it wasn't anything he could eat. "It's so light. I didn't expect that."

Ben pulled the camo netting down over the back end of the truck. "That's a good knife. It should last you a long time if you take care of it."

"I will." Allie stuffed the knife into her pocket.

They all got their backpacks on and Joel and Allie grabbed their weapons from where they had leaned them against a tree.

"Okay, let's do it," Ben said.

They walked single-file through the woods with Ben leading the way. Joel first, then Allie followed close behind. Gunner was doing his usual thing and running ahead, then back again to check in with everybody before racing ahead again.

"Easy, Gunner. Pace yourself, dog," Joel warned. But Gunner did a few more laps before he finally settled into a steady stride ahead of Ben.

"I think Gunner's leg is doing much better," Allie said.

When they got out of the woods, Ben walked to the edge of the interstate and looked back at where they'd driven the Blazer into the woods. The hard, dry ground showed no signs of tire tracks or anything else that would give up their hiding spot. No one would ever know the Blazer was tucked away back there. He hated to leave the truck and all their supplies, but they had no choice and it was hidden as well as it could be.

Satisfied that they hadn't left any sign of a trail, they headed back toward the wood line several yards off the road.

"Where are we going? Aren't we going to follow the road?" Joel asked.

"Yes, but I want to be close to the woods in case we hear somebody coming. That way we can be out of sight in a couple steps. I'm not really anxious to meet anybody else today," Ben answered.

"Good point," Joel said.

"It might be a little more trouble than walking on the shoulder of the road, but it will be a lot cooler and mostly in the shade," Ben added.

It was well after the hottest part of the day now, but that didn't seem to make a difference in the temperature. The shade along the edge of the woods provided little relief, and after the first couple of miles they decided to stop and rest. Everybody found a place to sit and there was silence as they all guzzled down some much-needed water.

"Do you hear that?" Joel asked. It sounded like running water. He got up and wandered into the woods a few yards. Gunner got up right away and followed him.

Ben and Allie joined him a few seconds later. They walked for several yards before they caught up to Joel, who was standing over a small running creek that wound its way through the woods. It was small enough to step across, but the water was clear and inviting.

They all stood there for a minute as if they didn't believe it was real. But Gunner proved otherwise as he splashed his way across to the other side before anybody could think to stop him.

"Oh, Gunner!" Allie shook her head. "So much for keeping the bandage dry!"

Gunner stopped lapping at the water for a second and looked up at Allie.

"It'll dry out in no time with this heat," Ben said.

"The water looks clean. Cleaner than anything we've seen since Colorado." Joel kneeled down and stuck his hand in the creek. "Oh, it's cold, too."

He set his gun down and used both hands to scoop water onto his face. Ben and Allie joined him a few seconds later.

"That feels really good." Allie rubbed the water over her arms and face.

"It must be spring-fed." Ben dipped his face down to the stream and washed off the road grime. The coolness of the water washed over him and he perked up a little. He sat back on his heels, water still dripping off his face. "We should fill the bottles while we're here."

"Do we need to filter it if it's spring-fed?" Joel asked.

Ben nodded. "Yeah, it looks good and would probably taste fine, but you always need to filter or boil water. No exceptions."

Joel got started filling bottles, and they all enjoyed the cool water and the shade for a few more minutes. At least until they heard the distant sound of a vehicle approaching.

· 2 ·

"Listen. I hear a car coming," Ben said.

Joel and Allie stopped filling bottles to pay attention. Even Gunner quit lapping at the water and stood still as the noise grew louder.

Ben stayed hunched down and made his way up the small incline to the edge of the woods so he could see the road. Careful to keep out of sight, he lay down in the pine needles and leaves as he waited.

It didn't take long for the noise to manifest itself into a light green Ford station wagon complete with fake wood panels. The wagon was meandering back and forth across the highway with what appeared to be no real purpose as it made its way closer to them. It was coming from the direction of Cloverdale, where Ben was hoping to find a part for the Blazer.

Joel belly-crawled up behind his dad. "See it yet?"

"Yeah. It's an old station wagon," Ben whispered

back. Allie stayed down by the creek with Gunner and hung on to his collar to keep him from following Joel up the embankment. Joel got up to where his dad was and lay next to him as they watched the car slowly approach.

"What are they doing?" Joel asked.

"I have no idea. I just hope they keep moving," Ben answered.

He noticed how slow the guy was going the closer he got. The driver was an older man wearing a ball cap, and no one else was in the car with him. Ben could see that the back of the wagon was piled high with mostly unidentifiable junk and a few boxes. Some of the things looked like car parts to Ben, but he couldn't be sure.

The old man was looking around as he drove and appeared to be searching for something or someone. When the station wagon passed their position, the older man driving leaned out the window and slowed down even more to look at something on the road.

Ben thought he was going to stop for a second and began to tense up. He was about to tell Joel to slide back a little when the wagon accelerated and moved on. Apparently, whatever he was looking at wasn't worth stopping for. To Ben, it seemed like the guy was scavenging.

Once the wagon had passed and was out of sight, Ben got up and brushed himself off.

"Well?" Allie asked.

"Just an old station wagon with a guy driving. He's gone now." Joel got off the ground and knocked a few pine needles off his shirt.

"He must be out scavenging the wrecks," Ben added.

The old guy must live around here somewhere. They'd have to keep an eye out in case he came back this way. Ben thought over the merits of trying to stop him if he did. If he was still alone, it might be worth trying to get a ride to Cloverdale from the man. Maybe he even knew where they could get a fuel pump for the Blazer.

Ben and the kids made quick work of topping off the water bottles and were back hiking alongside the road in just a few minutes. The sun was finally starting to relent as it sunk lower on the horizon behind them and began to fall below the tops of the trees.

The shade was a welcome relief, but it was a bittersweet consolation. Ben knew that it also meant the likelihood of getting back on the road today was slipping away fast. They still had a couple miles to go before they reached Cloverdale. And even if they got lucky and found the part they needed, they still had to get back to the truck and get it installed.

The Blazer was well hidden in the woods, but installing the part in the dark would mean the need for headlamps and flashlights. And that would give away their location to anyone passing by on the interstate. They had seen fewer and fewer people and cars on the roads the farther east they traveled over the last few days, but Ben didn't want to risk it.

Now that he thought about it, he couldn't help but wonder why there were fewer people and cars on the road the last day or so. They hadn't seen a lot of cars prior to that, but there was still the occasional car or truck on the road.

And in the towns they'd passed through, the number of people out and about had also diminished. Ben attributed most of this to the simple fact that supplies were scarce and a lot of people probably had given up at this point. Some people he was sure had no choice and were too weak to venture out any longer in search of food or water.

But still, he'd expected to run into a lot more people as they crossed the country and entered more densely populated areas. It was eerie, and at times he felt like they were the last people on earth.

Gunner was bringing up the rear and lagged several paces behind Allie. He was beginning to walk with more of a limp now and was putting less and less pressure on his injured leg. Ben was concerned, and Allie noticed him looking back at Gunner.

"I don't think he's got much more in him today," Allie said.

Ben stopped walking and let the kids catch up to him. Joel and Allie stopped when they got to where Ben was standing and they all waited for Gunner to join them. He hobbled the last couple paces and sat down at Allie's feet immediately after he reached them.

"Yeah, I'm not sure how much longer he can walk." Joel bent down and joined Allie as she rubbed Gunner. "Poor guy."

Ben sighed as he looked around. He thought about throwing the eighty-five pound dog over his shoulders for a while and letting Joel carry his pack, but he knew that would only be a temporary solution. He couldn't carry Gunner that far. He just didn't have it in him.

Allie pulled out the collapsible bowl from her bag and poured some water into it. Gunner sniffed at it and licked at the water half-heartedly. But he was more interested in lying on the ground and soon resumed that position. Ben weighed their options as he realized they weren't going to make it to town at this rate.

The most realistic thing he could think of was to make an improvised stretcher out of some branches and a roll of cordage in his bag. It was obvious Gunner wasn't going to make it any farther without help. And if they wanted to get to

Cloverdale before nightfall, they would have to do something now.

Ben was about to send the kids into the woods to get the necessary wood to build the stretcher, but just as he opened his mouth, Allie interrupted him.

"It's coming back," she said.

· 3 ·

Sure enough, Ben heard what sounded like the station wagon coming back down the highway in their direction.

"Joel, you and Allie get to the woods with Gunner."

"What are you gonna do?" Joel asked.

"I'm going to see if I can get us a ride. Just be ready if it goes bad and I need backup."

"Got it." Joel nodded and he and Allie headed for the wood line.

"Gunner, come!" Joel commanded.

Gunner reluctantly got up with a grunt and did his best to keep up with the kids as they jogged off the road and into the trees.

Ben hoped and prayed he wasn't making a huge mistake. But what choice did they have? They were running out of options. Even with the makeshift stretcher, it would be a slow-going and arduous last couple miles into town.

With any luck, the guy would still be alone. If things did go badly, Ben could most likely handle him one on one. Still, he wasn't one to underestimate anyone's capabilities, and he wasn't about to start now.

He dropped his pack to the ground and laid the M24 across the top. He repositioned his concealed carry holster from his hip to the small of his back and pulled his T-shirt over it. As he stood there waiting, he thought back to Durango and the day this had all happened.

He thought about how he and Joel had gotten a ride to their house from Dale. In that moment, he wondered about old Dale and his rusty pickup. Ben hoped the man was able to find his family and get out of Durango. But even more so, Ben hoped they could get a ride from this guy in the station wagon. Would he even stop?

As the ancient Ford got closer, Ben saw that it was just the one guy they had spotted before. There was no going back now. He'd surely been seen by the driver now as there was nothing between them but an open stretch of asphalt. Ben waved his arms over his head in an attempt to signal the guy without seeming too aggressive.

The wagon slowed and stopped about 40 yards away on the other side of the road. The man stayed in the car and kept it running while he eyeballed Ben and the surrounding area. Finally, the door opened and the man stepped out. He remained on his side of the car as his gaze shifted from Ben to the woods and then back again.

"Hello," Ben called out.

The man didn't answer at first. Instead, he opened the rear passenger's side door on his side of the car and pulled something out. Ben resisted the urge to draw his gun but his muscles tensed in anticipation of a conflict.

The man proceeded to walk around the front of the station wagon and Ben saw what he was carrying. Cradled in his hands was what looked like a 12-gauge pump shotgun. He held the gun loosely at his side and didn't aim it at Ben.

Ben kept his arms at his sides, making sure to keep his right hand a little closer to the side and center of his back. It was as close to the Glock as he dared move his hand without risking escalating the situation any further.

"What are you doing out here?" the man asked.

"I'm not looking for any trouble. We had some car issues a few miles back and we're trying to get to Cloverdale to look for parts," Ben explained.

The man walked closer, and all Ben could think was that he had made a terrible mistake trying to reason with the guy. They should have taken their chances with the stretcher and walked the rest of the way. The man now stood fewer than 10 feet away from him and was still holding the shotgun at his waist.

Suddenly, the man's demeanor changed as he raised the shotgun and rested it over his shoulder, barrel toward the sky.

"Army, huh?" the man asked as he looked at Ben's arm.

Ben looked down at his left arm and saw the man looking at his tattoo. The bottom half of the shield and lightning bolt with the word "ranger" protruded from under his sleeve.

"Yes, sir," he replied.

The man smiled and pulled up the arm of his T-shirt to reveal a tattoo on his shoulder. It was old and faded but Ben could make out a screaming eagle with the words "101st airborne" written on a banner below it.

"Nam." The old guy cleared his throat and extended his hand toward Ben. "Vincent, but my friends call me Vince, although I don't seem to have many left these days," he huffed.

Ben took his hand. "Ben Davis. Glad to meet you."

"Sorry about all that. You can't be too careful these days, you know." Vince shuffled his shotgun to his left hand and let it hang by his side.

Ben nodded. "I know what you mean. No offense taken."

Ben turned back to the woods and motioned for the kids to join him. Joel, Allie, and Gunner emerged from the vegetation one by one. "This is my son Joel and his friend Allie."

Before Joel or Allie could make their way over to shake Vince's hand, Gunner hobbled over to him faster than Ben had seen him move in a while. Gunner let out a few sharp barks and growls as he approached Vince, but his tail gave away his true intentions as it wagged with approval.

"And this is Gunner, who had a little run-in with a wolf the other night. Don't let the attitude fool you—he's friendly," Ben said.

"A wolf?" Vince seemed surprised. "Don't see too many of those around here, but I guess they're out there."

Gunner continued his approach to Vince and, after circling him a few times, finally settled down enough to receive a few scratches behind his ears from the old man.

Joel and Allie walked up and offered their hands to Vince, who took both in turn.

"Hi, I'm Joel."

"And I'm Allie. Nice to meet you."

"Pleasure to meet you all. So you had some car trouble, did you?" Vince looked back at Ben.

"Yeah. Fuel pump went up, I think. At least I hope it's only the fuel pump. We hid the truck a few miles back in the woods."

"I was going to ask because I didn't see anything new on the road. I travel this route almost daily, looking for parts and things. You wouldn't believe some of the things you come across out here."

"Oh, I believe you. We've seen it all since we left Colorado," Ben remarked.

"Wow. Colorado. That's a long haul. Where you headed?" Vince asked.

Joel spoke up. "Maryland to get my mom and brother and sister."

"But first, Pittsburgh, to get my dad," Allie added.

The smile left Vince's face for a moment when Allie spoke, and he looked like he was going to say something to her but stopped and looked at Ben. "Well, that's quite the trip. I think I can help you guys get back on your way. I run a garage in Cloverdale. Well, I used to. Nowadays I pretty much just scavenge what I can find and run a bit of a trading post. What kind of vehicle you drivin'?"

"My son's '72 Chevy Blazer," Ben answered.

Vince looked at Joel. "Oh, nice. A classic. Of course, I guess they're all classics now." He chuckled to himself. "I have an old Chevy van with a blown transmission in the yard behind my shop. I believe the fuel pump off that ought to work in the Blazer."

"We're more than happy to pay you for your trouble," Ben offered.

"No trouble. Let's get you guys back to town so you can rest up and we'll take a look at that van. I have a spot for you guys to use to get cleaned up and spend the night if you like. We can come get your Blazer in the morning if that's all right with you. The highway is no place to be at night. We've been having problems with bandits out here and found it's best to stay in town." Vince began walking back to his station wagon.

Ben and the kids followed him, Gunner dragging behind once more.

"Come on, boy, just a little farther," Joel promised.

"Yeah, I think it will be all right until morning." Ben really didn't want to leave the Blazer overnight, but it was hidden well, and if Vince was willing to help out, he wasn't going to say no.

Ben was a decent mechanic and there wasn't much he and Joel couldn't fix, but if Vince was a trained mechanic, even better. What if it turned out to be more than a fuel pump? It would be nice to have an expert set of eyes take a look at it. Besides, if they were still traveling, it was already getting late in the day and was about the time they'd be stopping to make camp anyway. Vince hadn't mentioned what type of accommodations he had for them, but it couldn't be any worse than sleeping on the ground.

Joel and Allie helped Gunner onto the back seat while Vince moved a few things out of their way.

"Sorry about that. It's a little junky back there. I wasn't planning on any passengers today." He moved a few car batteries off the seat and put them in the back with the rest. He must have had a dozen batteries in the back along with a few other random parts that he had collected.

Joel and Allie loaded in their bags and weapons, then climbed in after Gunner and sat on the now-empty bench seat.

"I really can't tell you how much we appreciate this," Ben said.

"It's no trouble really. I'm glad to help you guys out," Vince reassured him. Once everyone was in the station wagon, he put the car in gear and pulled out. He picked up speed and surprised Ben with the old wagon's quickness.

"She ain't pretty, but she's got it where it counts." Vince laughed and sped up even more as the engine roared to life. "So Colorado, huh? You've seen a good bit of the country then, I guess. What's it like out there? I haven't ventured out farther than 10 or 15 miles from town in any direction since it all went down."

"It's pretty rough. People are desperate and willing to do anything. We've run into our share of bad guys out there," Ben answered.

"Boy, that's a shame. It's really brought out the worst in some people. I think you'll be pleasantly surprised when we get to Cloverdale. We've managed to keep things pretty civil."

"We?" Ben asked.

"Oh yeah, there's quite a few of us gettin' by in town. Those of us that survived the fires have combined our resources and are trying to keep things as normal as possible."

"What do you mean by that? Survived the fires?" Ben asked.

"Well, when the EMPs hit, a lot of places burned down. It must have caused electrical surges and things went haywire," Vince answered.

"Yeah. We've seen a lot of that," Ben agreed.

"Well, most of the population died from that. At least in our town they did. At that hour of the morning, most folks were in bed. With no smoke alarms or smoke detectors in operation, a lot of people never woke up. And they were the lucky ones. We lost a lot of people from severe burns and smoke inhalation in the days that followed. There's about 30 of us left." Vince's face was serious now, and Ben knew what he'd meant before about not having many friends left.

Ben saw the exit up ahead, and Vince began to slow down as he approached the curve of the ramp.

He grinned. "Almost home."

· 4 ·

As they rounded the curve of the exit ramp, Ben saw what looked like a row of brand-new Cadillacs and Chevys lined up across the road. The cars extended off in both directions and formed a wall that curved back to connect to buildings on both sides of the road. The wall of cars created an impenetrable barrier and ran between the buildings that remained standing.

"You like it? Courtesy of the local car dealership. We've got about 10 acres inside the wall and a gate on both sides. Only way in or out, at least by car," Vince said.

Ben nodded. "Impressive."

It was a strange sight, for sure, to see the mostly pristine vehicles crudely lined up. There were even a few Corvettes in the mix, bumper to bumper with the Escalades and Suburbans. That was all they were really good for anymore. The EMPs had reduced the high-dollar cars and trucks to nothing more than a movable barricade.

A man with a rifle stood in the bed of a Dodge pickup truck. The truck was parked on the inside of the wall of cars at an entrance point on the road in. When the man saw the wagon coming, he jumped down and got in the Dodge and positioned himself behind a brand-new Suburban that still displayed its paperwork in the driver's side window. He proceeded to push the shiny black SUV out of the way, making an opening for Vince to drive through.

Vince waved at the guy as they drove through. "That's Bill. He and his wife and their little girl were a few of the lucky ones. They lost their house but made it out alive. They've moved into town here like the rest of us. Most folks have been sleeping in the local motel. I got the place hooked up with a power supply that we use sparingly for a few hours at night and when needed."

"Welcome back, Major." Bill gave a casual salute as he hung out of the window of the old Dodge pickup. As soon as they were inside the wall of cars, Bill drove around to the front of the Suburban and pushed it back into place with his truck, closing off the entrance.

"I guess you could say I'm the unofficial mayor in town." Vince grinned. "And on that note, welcome to Cloverdale."

Ben noticed on the way through the wall of cars that, on the outside, the cars were dented and scratched in a few places and some of them sported more than a couple bullet holes.

He looked at Vince. "You've been having a lot of trouble here from outsiders?"

"Yeah, but nothing we haven't been able to handle so far. We all take turns standing watch, and so far, we've been able to stay one step ahead of them. In addition to people at the gates, we always have at least two others patrolling the wall perimeter 24-7. It makes for a busy watch schedule, but we manage. Not that we have a choice."

As they drove farther into the town, Ben immediately noticed that most of the stores still had the windows intact and hadn't been looted or robbed. He glanced back at the kids and saw they were looking out windows, probably as shocked as he was to see a semi-normal-looking streetscape. The only indicator that things weren't as they should be was the missing people and the occasional burned-down structure.

"You guys have done a good job here. It almost looks normal," Ben said.

"Thanks. It hasn't been easy. I guess you've seen worse, huh?"

"A lot worse! Some places are completely destroyed. St. Louis is gone. We didn't get that close, but there was no need to. The smoke was still rising when we passed."

Vince's expression changed to the same one

he'd had before, when Allie had mentioned Pittsburgh.

He swung the old wagon into a motel parking lot and parked at the front office. "One of the guys here in town is a ham radio nut and he was able to save his equipment. He's been able to get a little info here and there. The signals have been few and far between and mostly static. I can tell you what we know later, but right now, let's get you guys settled for the night. I'm sure you're exhausted."

Ben picked up on the notion that Vince didn't want to get into the details of what he knew in front of the kids. He took the hint and didn't push him for any more information. There would be time to talk later. Right now, he was looking forward to the prospect of getting cleaned up and lying down on an actual bed tonight.

They all followed Vince's lead and got out of the car with their gear.

"Are we going to stay here?" Allie's eyes grew wide with excitement.

"That's right. We've got a room with your name on it," Vince answered.

Allie looked around at Ben and Joel with a smile on her face.

"I'll be right back." Vince disappeared through the door to the motel's office and was back out in under a minute. He tossed a set of keys to Ben.

"Room 117 is all yours. Everything in the room will work from seven to nine tonight, so take advantage while you can. Except the TV, of course. After that, we shut it down."

"Even the water?" Allie bit her lip.

"Even the water. We have a natural spring in town not far from here and we managed to get the hotel's plumbing tied in." Vince gave her a smile, then turned to Ben. "Maybe after you get settled, come on over to the shop and see me. I'll check and see if we can use the fuel pump off that van. I'm right across the street." Vince pointed to a service station on the other side of the road from the motel.

"Thanks again," Ben said.

"Yes, thank you so much!" Allie said.

"Thank you!" Joel repeated.

Vince started to get back in his car when he stopped. "Oh, I almost forgot. The Morgans' daughter was going to college to be a veterinarian. She was home for the summer, visiting her folks, when it all went down. I'll see if I can catch up with them and have her swing by and look at your dog. Maybe there's something she can do for him."

Ben shook his head in disbelief. "Wow! And at the risk of sounding like a broken record, thank you again!"

Ben and Vince shook hands. Then Vince hopped in the wagon and was gone. The three of them and

Gunner stood there in the parking lot for a minute as they watched him drive across the street.

"Well, let's check out the room!" Joel headed for the row of doors under the covered walkway. Ben and Allie were right behind him as he counted off the room numbers.

"115, 116, 117. This is us." Joel stopped in front of the door. Ben handed him the keys and let him open it. He let Allie and Gunner in first, then followed them in.

Ben took another quick look up and down the street before he joined them inside the room.

Allie opened the curtains before anyone put their things down. The remaining light left in the evening flooded the room as it reflected off the dust particles in the air. The dim light cut through the otherwise dark room to reveal two double beds and a dresser with a TV on it. The room was dated and looked straight out of the '70s, complete with red shag carpet and wood paneling. The air was stale and had a musty smell to it, but compared to their normal accommodations, it felt like a five-star resort.

Even Gunner seemed to come to life a little as he sniffed his way around the room.

"What time is it?" Allie asked.

Ben checked his watch. "It's about a quarter to seven. You guys go ahead and use the bathroom first. I'm going to lie down for a minute." It was the most comfortable mattress he had ever felt in his life—or at least it seemed that way right now.

And as the fluffy down pillow enveloped his head, he closed his eyes and fell asleep.

· 5 ·

"Dad. Wake up, Dad." Ben opened his eyes to find Joel standing over him and shaking his arm. "Sorry to wake you but the bathroom is free now. I wanted to get you up before they turn the utilities off."

"Yeah...thanks." Ben sat up and stretched his arms out in front of him. He didn't remember falling asleep. Looking down at his watch, he saw that it was nearly 8:00. The curtains were still drawn back but there was no longer any light coming in from outside.

Allie was reading her book by a small lamp on the table between the beds. Gunner had found himself a spot next to her on the large bed and was sprawled out and snoring loudly.

Ben swung his legs over the side of the bed and rubbed his face for a second before he got up. He needed to get moving if he was going to take advantage of the amenities here before he went over to see Vince at his garage.

Just then there was a soft knock at the door. Gunner's head jolted upright, and he let out a sharp bark. Startled at Gunner's sudden outburst, Allie put her book down and sat up. Ben squinted as he focused through the peephole in the door. It was a young woman.

"It must be the vet student." Ben took the safety chain off the door and opened it slowly.

"Hi, I'm Reese." She stuck out her hand. "Vince sent me over to look at your dog if you want."

Ben shook her hand and stepped back to allow her easy access to the room. "Yes, please come on in. I'm Ben. That's Allie and my son, Joel."

The kids waved from where they were. Before Ben could introduce her to Gunner, the dog let out a whine, followed by a noise somewhere between a bark and a howl, as he sniffed in Reese's direction.

"Oh, settle down, boy." Allie rubbed his head in an effort to calm him.

"And that would be Gunner," Joel said.

Reese made her way to the bed and put her bag on the floor. She sat on the edge and let Gunner get familiar with her. He quickly warmed up to her and was wagging his tail in no time as she reached into her pocket and pulled out a treat. Gunner crunched loudly on the dry biscuit and then sniffed the bed for any pieces that might have fallen.

"So you're a veterinarian?" Ben asked.

"Well, I would have been next year. I'm a student at Cornell." She paused. "Was a student. Anyway, I'm the closest thing to a vet around here."

Ben smiled. "That's more than good enough for me!"

Reese began to unwrap the bandage on Gunner's leg as Allie tried to keep him calm and still. "What happened?"

"He was trying to protect me last night and got into a fight with a wolf," Allie answered.

"Oh my. A wolf, huh? What a brave boy you are!" Reese fawned over Gunner and rubbed him while she inspected the wound on his leg.

"We cleaned it and put some antiseptic gel on it before we wrapped it up. He was doing pretty well until we had to walk a few miles." Allie continually rubbed Gunner's head now.

"Well, it's a little swollen, but otherwise I'd say just keep doing what you're doing and it should heal up just fine. I don't see any infection and there are no broken bones. I can give him something for the pain. Just try to keep him off of it for a couple days if you can." She began going through her bag and pulled out fresh bandages and a few other things.

Ben glanced at his watch. "Well, if you guys have this handled and you don't mind, I'm going to get cleaned up before I run out of time."

"Oh, no problem. Go ahead. I can take care of this. Nice to meet you, Ben."

"Nice to meet you, too, Reese. And thanks for coming out tonight and having a look at Gunner."

"Glad to help out," she said.

Ben grabbed his bag and headed into the bathroom.

He was about to pull out his headlamp for light but stopped himself and tried the light switch. The bathroom filled with a pale yellow light and Ben got a good look at himself for the first time in a while.

He stared at his reflection in the mirror for a moment as he rubbed at the gray hairs taking over his beard. He reached over and turned the water on in the shower and was surprised to see it pour out of the showerhead. He half-expected it not to work, but sure enough, there was soon a stream of warm water splashing off the tiles.

Ben enjoyed the shower thoroughly and was careful not to spend too much time in there. He could have easily stood under the warm, clean running water for much longer, but part of him felt a little guilty about using more than his share of resources.

What they had going on here was impressive, and it was refreshing in and of itself that they were doing so well in this little pocket. It also gave him hope for the future. There were bound to be more places like this where the better qualities of human nature had prevailed. Not everyone had regressed into a state of chaos and malevolence.

Reese had gone and Gunner's leg had a fresh white bandage on it by the time Ben came out of the bathroom. The TV was on the floor, and in its place was one of the small gas-fired camp stoves. There was already a pot of water boiling, and Allie had a packet of dehydrated food in her hand.

"Don't worry. I opened the window," Joel said.

Ben was about to ask that very question after he saw the stove going. He really needed to start giving the kids more credit when it came to being responsible.

"I wasn't worried. You're a smart kid." He smiled. "Thanks for getting dinner started, but I don't want to keep Vince waiting. I'll have to eat when I get back." Ben hated to run out. It was late and he was starving, but he didn't want to come off as ungrateful for Vince's hospitality by making him wait around any more than he already had. He was also anxious to hear the information Vince had been so reluctant to share in front of the kids.

He grabbed a Clif Bar from his bag to stave off the hunger pains in his stomach and put his headlamp on. "I'll be back as soon as I can. Make sure you keep the door locked."

"Got it," Joel replied.

· 6 ·

Ben headed out across the parking lot and looked up and down the street. There weren't any people out and about, but he did notice a few windows with the faint glow of lights inside. Everyone was probably enjoying the last few minutes of electricity.

As he ate the Clif Bar, he wondered if all the remaining houses had water as well. From what he'd seen so far, he wouldn't be surprised. Even the streets were clean here compared to what they had seen in their travels. They were completely absent of any abandoned or wrecked vehicles. And any structures that had burned down inside the wall had been cleaned up and the debris pushed into neat piles out of the way.

Ben took his headlamp off and stuffed it into his back pocket. The moon was bright enough to light the way across the street to the service station. It was a small white building with a sign out front that read Major's Auto Repair. There were a couple of gas pumps out front and a four-bay garage on the side of a small storefront. One of the large overhead garage doors was open, and he could see a faint light coming from inside the building.

"Hello. Vince, you in here?" Ben called while he knocked on the frame of the open door.

"Back here," a voice answered.

Ben followed the light back to an office, where he found Vince sitting at a desk.

"Have a seat. Relax." Vince motioned to the chair that sat opposite his desk in the cramped room. The old lounge chair showed its age with stuffing poking out through a few cracks in the dried and worn leather upholstery. But it was comfortable and it felt good to sit. The walls in the office were lined with shelves that were filled with books and automotive manuals adding to the overall crowded feeling of the space.

"Nice little business you got here," Ben commented.

"It was." Vince snorted and slid something across the desk at Ben. It was a replacement fuel pump for the Blazer.

"You found one!" Ben said.

"Yep. The van out back had a good one in it. That should work without any trouble in a '72 Blazer. We can slip out to your truck in the morning and get it swapped in no time. I'm sure you're anxious to get back on the road."

"As much as we appreciate your hospitality here, we really do need to keep moving. We're not nearly as far along as I'd hoped we'd be by now. Of course, we've had our share of setbacks since we started out over a week ago. Otherwise, Vince, I'd be very tempted to spend a day here and recharge. You guys have a good thing going here. You've really done a nice job of keeping things together." Ben played with the fuel pump in his hand.

He was eager to get as much information from Vince as he could, but he didn't want to seem pushy.

"Well, it hasn't been easy. That's for sure. I can't take all the credit, though. We've always been a tight-knit community. But to be honest, the first few days after the bombs, it was total chaos around here. Of course, I imagine it was in most places."

"From what we've seen, it still is." Ben shook his head.

"That bad, huh?" Vince paused and seemed to look past Ben for a moment. Then he opened a drawer in the desk and pulled out two small glasses and a bottle of whiskey.

Before Ben could object, he noticed the expression on Vince's face had changed. His brow was wrinkled with a look of concern and sincerity. He poured a healthy amount into each glass and slid one across the rough wooden surface of the desk toward Ben.

Vince held up his glass. "To Maryland," he said.

The last thing Ben wanted was a shot of whiskey on an empty stomach, but he felt obliged. After all, the guy had really come through for them in a big way. The least Ben could do was join him in a drink. One soldier to another.

Ben raised his glass. "Don't forget Pittsburgh." He followed Vince's lead and downed the drink. The warm liquid washed over his tongue and burned his throat as he swallowed the generous portion in a single gulp.

Vince looked at Ben. "About Pittsburgh." He stopped and shook his head, looking away and then back at Ben. "I don't know if it's true or not, but I've heard Pittsburgh is gone. I didn't want to say anything in front of the kids."

"What do you mean 'gone'?" Ben asked.

"I'm not sure what you've heard, so stop me if this is nothing new. But North Korea and Syria were behind the attacks. It was a combined effort, with Syria running interference from the inside. They installed a virus into the National Missile Defense System while the North Koreans launched ICBMs from offshore locations on both coasts. Their intentions were high-altitude detonations all over the U.S. We did manage to launch a counterstrike, but our systems went down before we confirmed any detonations. I can only imagine the North Koreans and unfortunately many of their neighboring countries are probably in worse shape than we are. I don't know if any other countries got in on the action, but I find it hard to believe they didn't. There were rumors of a possible Russian attack while our defenses were down. But I think that's more speculation than fact, although it would make sense now that we've bombed each other back to the Stone Age."

"So far that goes along with what we've heard, all except the counterattack and the Russian involvement," Ben said.

"That's pretty much what I know, except..." Vince paused and filled the glasses again. "Except not all of the nukes detonated like they were supposed to."

He didn't wait for Ben to join him this time and downed the glass of amber liquid quickly before continuing. "Some of them went off at lower altitudes. I hear some places are completely wiped off the map. Places like Pittsburgh."

Ben swirled the liquor around in the glass as he held it in his hand. He was trying to come to terms with the information Vince had just dumped in his lap and process how this was going to affect them. His first thought was of Allie and how this most likely meant that she had also lost her dad. This would devastate her. Now he felt like he needed the drink and willingly swallowed the contents of his glass.

Vince shrugged. "It might not be as bad as they say. Keep in mind, this information is coming from a bunch of old farts like me who play with ham radios for fun. You know as well as I do what happens to information after it's been passed down the line for a while. It tends to become exaggerated and distorted. There hasn't been any official broadcast that I know of. On top of all that, the incoming signals on the radio have been sporadic at best, with heavy interference."

"Were any other cities hit like that? Like Pittsburgh?" Ben winced as the alcohol burned his throat.

"I heard San Francisco, Houston, Atlanta, and D.C. were all hit pretty hard. The National Guard and FEMA set up camps in some of the bigger cities, but they're overwhelmed and can't handle the number of people demanding supplies. Also heard a few of the units have pulled out and it's every man for himself in some places. The government is in full-blown damage control at this point. I wouldn't expect a return to order anytime soon."

"Yeah, we saw a convoy headed to Denver. I picked up on a little radio chatter, but they were keeping it to a minimum. Wait. Did you say D.C.?" Ben leaned forward and put his glass on the desk.

"Yeah, is that near where you're headed in Maryland?" Vince went to pour them another round of drinks, but Ben quickly covered his glass with his hand and stopped him.

His head was already spinning, although he wasn't sure if it was from the whiskey on an empty stomach or from the new information he was getting and the horrible truth he knew about Allie's dad and the realization he was going to have to share that with her sooner rather than later.

ᐧ7ᐧ

Ben forced himself to reply.

"No. My kids are a few hours from there. But we have to go pretty close to D.C. to get to where they are in Maryland." Ben hadn't been looking forward to getting through the Baltimore-D.C. area as it was. Now he wondered if they should even try. If they couldn't get through, they'd have to go around the Chesapeake Bay to the north or south. And that would add at least another day to their trip.

"Hey, what time is it?" Vince asked.

Ben was caught off guard by the odd question and took a second to answer. "Ah… About a quarter after nine."

"Oh, well, I guess everybody got a few extra minutes tonight. Come on. Walk with me. I'll show you my power system." Vince got up from his desk and headed out into the workshop.

Ben followed as he led them through the garage bay to a steel door in the back. He watched as

Vince unlocked the heavy door with a key from his pocket.

Once inside the room, he flipped a switch. An old fluorescent ceiling fixture flickered to life, revealing what must have been no less than a couple hundred car batteries. They were all neatly stacked on wooden shelving that ran from the floor to the ceiling, all the way around the room. In the far corner was a series of six panel boxes linked together by steel conduit. The last panel box in the series had a large black cable that ran out through the concrete wall.

"Watch your step," Vince cautioned as he pulled down a gas lantern that was hanging on a nail by the door. He got the lantern primed up and lit the wick, playing with it until he was satisfied with the way it was burning.

"Here you go. We're going to need that in just a second." He then sauntered over to the last panel box and opened the cover. He threw a few switches and the ceiling light quickly faded until the fluorescent tubes were dark once more.

The only light in the room now was coming from the lantern in Ben's hand.

"I have them all hooked to solar panels on the roof. Most days, I can charge the batteries enough to give us a few hours of modern conveniences at night. I only turn it on for a couple hours, though, so we have a little power left in reserve for emergencies."

"This is quite a system you've got here." Ben looked around the room as he held the lamp up in the air. He was impressed with the mini power grid and, for a few seconds, forgot about the bad news.

"Thanks. It ain't pretty, but it works. Plus, I think it helps keep everybody sane around here. A few creature comforts and a hot shower make all the difference." Vince smiled.

"It's a good motivator. That's for sure," Ben agreed as they stepped out of the room and Vince locked the door behind them.

"I won't keep you much longer. I know you're tired. I just wanted to show you one more thing before you head back." Vince took the lamp from Ben and led the way once more through the garage bays, past the little office where they had talked earlier.

They stopped at another locked door. This one opened into the front section of the building housing the store. Vince led the way in, and as the lamplight carved into the shadows, sparsely loaded shelves came into view.

"I don't know how you guys are fixed on supplies, but I have a pretty good selection of stuff in here." Ben's eyes were immediately drawn to a large bag of rice and a small carton of canned dog food.

"Of course, we don't take cash or credit," Vince joked.

Ben smiled back. "I might have a few things you'd be interested in, too."

"Well, then tomorrow morning, after we get your truck running, you can follow me back here and take a look around. It'll give you guys a chance to top off your water and fill the truck with gas," Vince offered.

"I really do appreciate it. I mean, everything you've done. It's nice to know there are still good people out there. I guess we broke down in the right place," Ben said.

"No problem," Vince said. "We've got to stick together if any of us are going to make it."

Ben tried to fight off a yawn as he looked around at the items on the shelves. A small pile of potatoes sat on the table. He nodded. "We'll definitely come back and take a few things off your hands."

"Good. Now go and get some rest. I'll come get you bright and early."

"Sounds good. I'll see you then." Ben was tired and anxious to get back, but now it was the bed that was calling him, not the food. He'd lost his appetite the moment he heard about Pittsburgh.

They shook hands and said good night.

Ben headed back across the street, his mind playing through the conversation he was going to have with Allie. He could imagine her reaction, and the thought of it all made him cringe.

He turned around, startled from his thoughts, when Vince closed the big steel rolldown garage door and locked up. The sound echoed down the dark, empty street. There were no more lights in the windows now and the hotel was quiet.

Several of the other rooms had lights on when he'd left, and he wondered how many people were staying there. These people were lucky not to be out in the wasteland. This town was fortunate to have a guy like Vince, and Ben was sure that without him, this place would look like all the rest they'd been through.

How lucky had they been to cross paths with him? Ben couldn't help but wonder if it was good karma for cleaning up a few messes on their way here, if there was such a thing.

He was definitely going to mark this place down on his map. This would be a great spot to stop on their way back across the country. Plus, he liked the place. The people they'd met were friendly and, most importantly, civil.

This place restored his faith in humanity a little. There were good pockets of people out there that would come together and survive—thrive even. Life would always be a struggle; that was clear. He doubted he would ever see anything again that resembled a normal society in his lifetime.

But there was hope for Joel and Allie and Bradley and Emma. There was reason to believe they would all have some of their old lives back someday.

By the time Ben got to the room, he was in a pretty good mood. Maybe it was the whiskey. Maybe it was the lack of sleep. But he decided to wait and talk to the kids tomorrow about what he had learned. At least they would get a good night's sleep, and Allie would have a better time coping with the news if she was well rested and fresh tomorrow.

Not that any amount of rest could prepare her for what he had to tell her.

· 8 ·

Joel sat up in bed with a start.

He wasn't sure if it was a dream or if he had heard an air horn go off in the distance. The next short blast confirmed that it was real, and it also woke his dad up, who was lying next to him on the bed.

He looked at Allie, who was still asleep on the other bed. Gunner was curled up next to her but was now also sitting up and listening to the commotion outside. He heard a door slam a few rooms down, followed by the sound of muffled voices.

Ben scrubbed a hand over his face. "What's going on?"

"I don't know. I just woke up," Joel answered. They both looked over as Allie began to stir now.

"What is it?" She wiped at her eyes.

"Something's happening outside." Ben was already up and putting his shoes on.

"Where are you going?" Joel asked, still half asleep.

"To find out what's going on. You guys stay here but be ready in case we need to move." Ben grabbed his M24 and slung it over his shoulder as he slipped out the door.

The door slammed with a thud, and the room was suddenly quiet again as Joel and Allie sat there and came to terms with their rude awakening.

She sighed. "So much for getting a good night's sleep. What time is it anyway?"

"I don't even know." Joel rubbed his eyes and looked out the window. The moon was close to where it had been when he was last awake. He and Allie had fallen asleep last night before his dad got back. He didn't remember much after noticing Allie had dozed off and remembered staring up at the moon from his bed before he fell asleep.

"I don't think we've been asleep for very long," he said.

Just then, he heard footsteps coming down the walkway outside. It sounded like people running. The footsteps turned into shadows outside the window, and two figures passed the room quickly. The sound of running and frantic voices faded quickly into the night.

"We better get our stuff together. Something big is going on."

Joel and Allie began to put everything away that

they had gotten out the night before. He was hoping to have a more leisurely exit and grew more concerned as he hastily stuffed his bag.

It didn't take long to get packed up, and now there was nothing to do but sit and wait. For the first time since he'd met Allie, he couldn't think of anything to say. He got off the bed and paced the room, checking out the window with each pass. He couldn't see anything from the angle of the room to the street, which only made it worse. He wanted desperately to know what was going on, and he was worried about his dad.

"I wish he'd taken the radio so he could let us know what's happening," Joel said.

"Well, he was in a hurry. I'm sure he's fine," Allie responded.

Just then, the distant crack of a rifle broke the silence, startling them. Then again a few seconds later, only this time louder and much closer to the motel.

"That's it! I can't take it! I'm going out to see what's going on. He might need my help!" Joel grabbed the AR15 and started out the door.

"Joel, wait!"

But it was too late. Joel had made up his mind that he wasn't going to sit this one out. He paused to answer her. "Keep it locked and don't let anybody in here. I'll come back as soon as I know something."

Then he closed the door behind him, leaving Allie and Gunner in the room.

The street was dark and it was hard to make out what was going on, but Joel could see a few people running on the road and sidewalk. They were all headed in the same direction: past the motel and toward the gate where they had first entered through the wall of cars. His eyes began to adjust to the darkness, letting him see that everyone running past was carrying a gun.

He jogged to the sidewalk in front of the motel and looked down the street. Light gleamed at the end of the road. There were two spotlights on utility poles, one on each side of the street. They were positioned at the edge of the wall around the town and focused out on the road leading into town. He hadn't noticed them yesterday when Vince had brought them here.

Engines revved in the distance now, followed by a few more gunshots.

He ducked down briefly, not sure what to do when he heard someone come up behind him. Before he could turn around, he heard a man's voice.

"Hey, new guy, come with me! They're trying to get in again." The man barely slowed his pace as he passed by Joel. "Come on!"

The guy was younger than Joel expected when he caught a glimpse of his face on the way by. Joel snapped out of it and bolted after him. "What's going on?" he called out.

"Same thing that happens just about every night. They try to get in and we try to keep 'em out."

"Who are they?" Joel huffed as he tried to keep up.

"They're a gang that runs the highway around here. They're the reason for the wall and why nobody goes outside it at night." The man slowed a little, and Joel caught up and jogged alongside him.

"Name's Cyrus, but most just call me Cy. I heard there were some new people in town that the major brought back with him yesterday."

"Yeah, my truck broke down a few miles from here and he gave us a ride yesterday. We're staying at the motel back there. I'm Joel, by the way."

"Well, welcome to Cloverdale, Joel, and keep your head down."

They finally reached their destination and crouched down behind the wall of cars. Joel noticed that every so often along the wall there was an area where sandbags were stuffed under the vehicles. The sandbags were stacked up to the quarter panels of the cars and trucks, blocking off the opening underneath the vehicles and the road.

It was at these spots that the people he had seen run past the hotel were gathered in small groups of two or three.

"Every night the same thing. That's why everybody goes to bed so early around here. You can count on getting up between 12:00 and 2:00 every morning and manning your post if you're an able-bodied person," Cy explained as he crouched behind the Suburban they were hiding behind and peered over the front fender.

Joel looked up and down the wall as it curved inward around the town. He studied the shadowy figures as they crouched at their post every 100 yards or so along the wall. He still hadn't seen his dad yet.

"Here they come again. Get down!" Cy sunk even farther below the hood of the large SUV.

Joel did the same, and just his eyes were above the hood now as he watched the road beyond the gate. He heard the truck coming long before he could make out what it was. It sounded like a big truck, as he could clearly hear the whine of the engine shifting gears.

Suddenly, two headlights cut through the darkness and a row of orange lights came on over the top of them.

It was an old red dump truck, and it was barreling toward the gate.

· 9 ·

The truck was a few hundred yards away from making impact when a single shot rang out from somewhere down along the wall.

Joel saw the bullet punch through the truck windshield in front of the driver. A spider web of cracks radiated out from the impact, quickly blocking out Joel's view of the driver. But Joel didn't need to see more to know that the bullet had found its mark.

The big truck immediately began to drift off the road and slow down as it rolled off the shoulder and into an open field. It finally stopped moving as it surrendered to the waist-high grass and weeds, its headlights still shining across the overgrown field.

"Yes!" Cy shouted. He was joined by a few whoops and hollers from farther down the wall.

"Finally, somebody got one of them. Look! They're scared now." He pointed to a distant group of headlights sitting back close to where the truck had come from.

Joel couldn't make out what kind of cars they were, but the count of headlights told him there were at least three other vehicles that had been with the dump truck. They stayed at a distance and were probably trying to figure out what to do now that their plan to ram their way into the gate had failed.

Another shot rang out from down the wall, and almost instantly, one of the six headlights exploded in a spray of glass. Within a few seconds, the cars were driving around in an unorganized fashion and seemed to be going in circles for a minute. They kicked up plumes of dust and gravel as the last car spun around and headed after the other two.

As soon as the last taillights disappeared into the darkness, three short blasts on the air horn sounded, startling Joel. "What was that for?"

"It just means that it's over," Cy replied.

A group of people now wielding flashlights and lanterns began gathering together in one central spot, back away from their posts along the wall. The small crowd formed into a circle, and Joel could hear some of them talking excitedly.

He followed Cy, and they made their way over to the group. When Joel got close, he saw his dad standing in the middle and fending off a barrage of back-patting and handshakes.

"Did you see that? What a shot," one older gentleman said as he shook Ben's hand.

"I bet they won't come back here for a while," a woman from the back of the crowd yelled.

"I wouldn't be too sure about that. They'll want revenge now," another man complained.

Vince spoke up as he slapped his hand on Ben's shoulder. "Well, we can't just let them walk in here and take what they want. What are we supposed to do, Bob? Fighting back is the only way we're going to survive, and now they know we mean business. Thanks to this man right here."

A young man not much older than Joel pushed his way through to the front of the group. "What type of gun is that, mister?"

"It's a .338 Lapua with a few small modifications," Ben answered.

The kid was about to say something else when Vince interrupted. "There will be plenty of time to talk tomorrow. Let's let these folks get some rest. Ben and I have some business to take care of early in the morning, but we'll be back for breakfast at the motel." He turned to face Ben. "You guys will stay and join us for breakfast, won't you? After all, you earned it tonight, my friend."

"You guys have done enough for us already. But it would be nice to have something other than oatmeal for a change," Ben admitted.

"We won't keep you long. It'll give you a chance to get squared away before you head out. A good meal and a tank of gas. You can't pass that up," Vince added.

"No, I guess we can't," Ben said.

Vince looked at a middle-aged woman in the crowd. "It's settled then. Mary, figure on three more tomorrow for breakfast."

"No problem, Major. Glad to have them." She put her hand on Ben's shoulder before beginning the walk back toward town.

The small crowd started to disperse, and Ben finally noticed Joel in the crowd. He shook his head. "I thought you were keeping an eye on things back at the room."

"I was, but I heard gunshots and got worried."

"So you left Allie?"

Joel shrugged. "I was worried about you. I wanted to help out."

He was tired of feeling helpless and wanted to get more involved in things. He wanted his dad to trust him enough to let him help. He wasn't a kid anymore, and he was tired of being treated like one. Sooner or later, his dad was going to have to accept that and give him more responsibility.

Cy, still next to Joel, stuck his hand out. "Hi, I'm Cy."

Ben smiled and shook Cy's hand before quickly looking back at Joel. All signs of the brief grin were gone and had been replaced with a scowl. "We'll discuss this later. I'm too tired to get into it now."

Joel was about to fire back, but Vince injected himself into the conversation. "I'll pick you up in the morning. First light, I'll have tools and coffee."

"Sounds good." Ben headed back to the room without saying a word to Joel.

Cy patted Joel on the back. "Let him get some rest. He'll forget all about it by morning. I'm sure you're all just tired, is all."

"You don't know my dad." Joel sighed.

Vince joined Joel and Cy on the walk back. "Your dad's in a tough position, Joel. He knows you're growing up fast. He just doesn't know how to let go yet. Then throw all this craziness into the mix. It's hard. Take it from someone who knows firsthand." And with that, Vince threw a playful punch into Cy's shoulder.

"Yeah, yeah. I hear you, Dad." Cy smirked.

As they walked, the three made small talk until Vince broke away and headed to the garage. "Got to shut the power down for the spotlights. Tell your dad thanks for his help tonight and thank you for coming out, too. He's lucky to have you. See you in the a.m."

"Will do," Joel said.

He and Cy continued on a little farther until they were standing on the street in front of the motel.

"Well, this is me. Thanks for not leaving me running around on the street like an idiot earlier." Joel laughed.

"Yeah, no problem. Hey, I should thank you for coming out to help. You could have stayed hidden in your room and nobody would have blamed you. We could use a few more guys like you and your dad around here."

"Maybe after we get my brother and sister in Maryland we'll swing back through here. You never know."

"Maybe. Well, good night. See you at breakfast." Cy waved and strode off down the street.

"Yep, good night." Joel walked across the parking lot to the motel building.

At least Cy and the major appreciated his help tonight. He wished his dad would see it that way. With any luck, his dad would be asleep and they could avoid hashing it out in front of Allie.

Joel didn't want to add embarrassment to his list of sins tonight.

· 10 ·

Ben was already awake when he heard the old station wagon pull up outside the motel room. He could have easily stayed in bed for much longer, but the fact that the Blazer was sitting out in the woods and needed repairs was more than enough motivation to get him moving.

He gathered his things from around the room quietly and tried not to wake the kids. Allie and Gunner were intertwined in a pile of blankets and sheets.

Without the use of the room HVAC unit, the room had grown hot and stale. The open window provided little in the way of ventilation, and the stillness of the morning air hung heavy in the room.

Ben placed his hand on Joel's shoulder and gave him a gentle shake. "I'm heading out. I'll be back as soon as I can," he whispered.

"Okay," Joel mumbled. He rolled over and buried his face in the pillow.

Ben grabbed his rifle and backpack from where he had left them by the door and slipped out. He pulled the door closed behind him and jiggled the handle to make sure it was locked.

Vince smiled at him through the windshield. True to his word, he had a hot cup of coffee waiting for Ben when he got in the car.

"Hope you had a good night's sleep. Well, at least after the craziness died down. That was some good shooting last night, I'll tell you." Vince backed the car out of the lot and headed for the gate.

"Well, I've had lots of practice lately," Ben said.

Vince waved at a man Ben recognized as one of the crew that had manned the wall last night. He moved the Suburban out of the way for them and made an opening in the wall of cars.

"Maybe those guys will give us a break for a while now. It'd be nice to sleep all the way through the night for a change. I guess they think they'll wear us down eventually." Vince's expression matched the exasperated tone of his voice. "I'm not sure how much longer we can hold out."

Ben couldn't think of anything to say. As he sat and drank his coffee, all he could focus on was getting the truck fixed and getting back on the road—that and the fact he was going to have to talk with Allie about Pittsburgh.

They passed the old dump truck that had

attempted to ram its way through the wall last night and Ben could see the driver's lifeless body still hunched over the wheel. His hands still gripped the wheel as if he would sit up at any moment and drive away. Ben forced himself to look away and tried to think about something else.

"Did you get a chance to talk with the kids about Pittsburgh last night?" It was like Vince had read his mind.

"No. I want to wait until we get on the road. I didn't want to ruin her night. They've both been through a lot."

"Yeah, I'm sure they have. Probably a good idea," Vince agreed.

Once they were back out on the road, Vince picked up speed, and before long, they were near where they had hidden the Blazer in the woods.

Ben pointed. "Right up there."

Vince slowed down and pulled across the dry, grassy median. He turned the wagon around to face the other direction before parking on the shoulder. They both got out, and while Ben gathered his bag and rifle, Vince pulled a small metal toolbox out of the back.

"I should have everything we need in here. This won't take too long. You'll be back on the road in no time and back for breakfast."

"Sounds good to me. I hope it's just the fuel pump," Ben said.

"If not, we can always tow it back to the shop and work on it there. There isn't anything that can't be fixed." Vince closed the tailgate on the wagon and put the window up. After the wagon was locked up, Ben led the way into the woods and back to the truck.

"Boy, you guys really did a good job of hiding the truck. I never would have known this was back here." Vince cleared a branch out of his way.

Ben smiled. "That was the idea."

"Your kids are lucky to have you, you know that?"

"That's funny, because I think I'm lucky to have them. Without them, there'd be no point to all this, would there?"

"No, I suppose not. Oh, the things we do for our kids!"

Ben was relieved to see the truck. The Blazer was just the way they had left it, and Ben could tell right away that nobody had messed with anything, let alone found it. He didn't waste any time pulling off the camouflage netting and exposing the vehicle.

"That's a nice-looking Blazer!" Vince admired the truck as he walked around to the front and set his toolbox down in the leaves.

Ben quickly unlocked everything and pulled the hood release. "Thanks. We had the engine rebuilt professionally, but Joel and I did most of the other stuff ourselves. She was a little rough when we got her."

"I've always liked these old Chevys." Vince lifted the hood and propped it open. He got right into the repair and had the old fuel pump off and set it on the bumper quickly. Then he turned to getting the new one installed. Vince did the work while Ben handed him what he needed. With Vince's expertise, the job was done in less than 45 minutes, and they were ready to fire up the engine and test the replacement pump.

Ben closed his eyes as he put the key in the ignition and cranked it. He didn't open them again until he heard the engine roar to life. The sound of the motor running smoothly brought a smile to his face. He revved it a few times and was glad to hear the consistent exhaust tone and lack of hesitation from the truck as he feathered the gas pedal.

Vince slammed the hood shut, and then he gave Ben a thumbs-up through the windshield.

While Vince cleaned up his tools, Ben hastily folded up the camouflage netting and stuffed it in the back of the truck.

"Hop in! I'll give you a ride back out to your car."

Vince put his toolbox on the passenger's side floor and climbed into the seat. Ben backed the Blazer all the way out of the woods, not bothering to turn around. He swung the wheel hard to the right, turned the truck onto the road, and stopped alongside Vince's wagon.

"I'll follow you back just in case you have any trouble." Vince opened his door and grabbed his toolbox.

"Thanks." Ben nodded. He waited for Vince to get loaded up and get his car started before he pulled out and headed for Cloverdale once more. He pushed the truck hard on the way back to town, thinking that if there were any other issues, now was the time to find them.

But the Blazer ran well, and before long, Vince was following him onto the exit and down the road. Ben looked for the dump truck but it was no longer parked in the tall grass where it had come to a rest last night.

As he approached the gate, the man who had been there earlier to let them out had been relieved, and there was a new face Ben didn't recognize. He waved as the man moved the Suburban to let him and Vince pass.

Once inside, he saw the dump truck parked off to the side. The body was gone now and the windshield had been removed.

He pulled into the motel parking lot and steered the Blazer into a spot right outside of their room. Vince pulled in and parked near the office, where he had dropped them off last night.

Ben left his bag and rifle in the truck and locked

it before he knocked on the motel door. He heard Gunner bark from inside, and a few seconds later, Joel opened the door. His hair was wet and Ben could smell the fresh scent of soap.

"Everything is on again," he said. "Allie is in the shower now. We figured we might as well take advantage. Who knows when we'll get the chance again." Joel shrugged.

"Yeah, that sounds like a good idea," Ben agreed.

Joel looked out the door as Ben entered the room and saw the Blazer parked outside.

"Yes! You got it fixed." Joel smiled.

"Vince did. I pretty much just watched. But it's running great now."

Just as Ben was getting ready to sit down on the edge of the bed, a knock came from the still-open door. He turned to see Mary from last night standing in the threshold.

Gunner let out a few grumbles and then started to wag his tail, not bothering to get up from the bed.

"Morning," Ben said.

"Morning," she answered. "Breakfast will be ready in about half an hour. But take your time. We're down in the motel conference room when you're ready. Bring the dog if he can behave himself." She smiled as she backed out of the doorway and was gone before he or Joel could respond.

Joel stuck his head outside and called out after her, "Thanks! We'll be there!"

Then he went to the bed, where Gunner was lying, and sat. Gunner rolled over just enough to expose his belly to Joel and shot him a pathetic look. Joel took the hint and gave him a few rubs.

"Listen, I'm sorry about last night," Ben started.

"No, it's my fault. I should have listened. I just wanted to help out. I feel so helpless sometimes." Joel shrugged.

"It's okay. We just need to be unified in our approach to any problems we encounter. And counting on each other to stick to the plan is important," Ben added.

"I know. I'm sorry," Joel said.

Ben smiled at Joel and was relieved to clear the air. He already felt guilty enough about the news he had to give Allie.

· 11 ·

Ben took a quick shower after Allie was done in the bathroom, and the kids packed their things in the Blazer while they waited for him.

Once they had cleared their things out of the room, they all made their way down the covered walkway, past the other rooms to the motel office. As soon as they entered, they were greeted with the smell of food. Through a set of double doors, they heard voices coming from down the hall. There were about a dozen people sitting around a rectangular table in the middle of the room, most of whom Ben had met briefly last night during the attack.

He was surprised to see the extent of the spread the townspeople had put on and he wondered if it was all on their account or if this was normal. He doubted that and thought it was probably an attempt to get them to extend their stay.

The kids were as wide-eyed as he was at the

food that was laid out on a long table against the wall. There were eggs, bacon, orange juice, pancakes, toast with butter and jelly, and what looked like fresh-baked muffins. Just about everything Ben expected to see at a typical breakfast buffet under normal circumstances.

Gunner was all nose as he wandered into the room and started to drool at the smells that filled the air. Ben could hear the dog inhaling deeply as he held his head up high and walked toward the table of food oblivious to his wounded leg.

"Wow!" Joel said.

Vince smiled from his seat at the head of the table, his plate already full with an assortment of food. "Help yourselves!"

"Thank you," Allie said as she took a plate from the end of the table.

Ben looked over the table of food as he got in line behind Joel. "This is quite the spread, Vince!"

"This is one of the perks of taking your turn standing watch at the wall, although I have to admit that this is a little more than we normally put out. Some of us here were hoping to entice you guys into extending your stay. No pressure, though. I told them all you're headed to Maryland." Vince glanced around the table at a few of the people.

"What? We could use the help." Reese, the almost veterinarian, shrugged.

"You know those lunatics will be back," another man added.

"All right. Let's let our guests eat in peace," Vince chimed in.

Ben was thankful for the silence and gladly took the opportunity to shove some much-needed food into his watering mouth. The group ate quietly for the next several minutes, except for the occasional small talk and the sound of silverware scraping plates.

Gunner was doing his best to control himself as he sat between Joel and Allie, licking his chops loudly.

"You can give the dog a little something if you want, hon." Mary nudged Allie's arm.

"Are you sure?" Allie asked.

"Yeah, go ahead. He looks pitiful and I'm sure he could use it. The poor thing! How did that happen?" She was looking at Gunner's leg.

"He put himself between me and a wolf the other day. Thanks to Gunner, I'm here to talk about it!" Allie put some bacon fat and eggs on a small paper plate before she put it on the floor in front of Gunner. He eagerly inhaled the food in a few seconds, after which he seemed to settle down and lay his head on the carpeted floor.

"He seems to be doing pretty good this morning," Reese said.

"Yes! Thank you for looking him over last night." Joel nodded.

"No problem. Glad to help." Reese smiled.

The major cleared his throat and pushed away from the table as he sat back with his coffee. "After breakfast, why don't you follow me over to the shop? We'll get your tank topped off with gas. Plus, you guys can have a look around and see if there is anything you need. You said you might have some things to barter with?"

Ben nodded and swallowed his mouthful of food. "Definitely!"

They finished eating and helped clean up the room before everyone slowly trickled outside to the parking lot. Cy had a couple plates filled with food stacked on top of each other in his arms.

"I'll run this out to the guys on watch," he said. "Nice to meet you guys, if I don't get a chance to see you before you take off."

They all said goodbye to Cy and then headed over to where the Blazer was parked.

The rest of the people dispersed one by one back down the street in different directions. Some returned to the motel where they were staying. Ben guessed those were the unlucky few who had lost their homes, or maybe their houses were outside the security of the wall.

Everyone was plenty friendly, but he could tell the late-night raids were taking their toll. They all had the look of someone who had been up too long and had been stressed out, although they hid it well. The bloodshot eyes and worried faces gave away the fact that they were running over capacity.

He felt a little guilty about the breakfast they had put out for them, sure now that it had been intended to lure them into staying here and helping out. He wished there was something more they could do to repay them for their kindness and generosity, but they had their own problems to deal with.

Joel lifted Gunner into the truck and Allie helped get him situated in the back seat before they all got in and drove across the street to the major's place.

As Ben pulled into the service station, Vince was waiting out front and directing him to pull in under the covered gas pumps.

"Any pump. They all work," Vince said.

Ben parked by the first one and turned the truck off. He and the kids got out, but Allie stopped Gunner from following them. "Sorry, boy, but you need to stay off that leg."

"Yeah, and you're too heavy to lift back into the truck anyway," Joel added, shaking his head.

Allie threw a few handfuls of dry dog food into a bowl and filled another with water. She put them both on the center console for him.

"Here you go, boy. We'll be right back." Allie rolled the window down and closed the door.

Vince already had the pump out of its cradle and was putting the nozzle into the truck.

"Well, this is a luxury," Ben said. "Fueling up is usually a little more involved."

"We're a full-service establishment!" Vince joked. "You kids feel free to have a look around inside."

Joel and Allie headed inside the small store that Ben had gotten a glimpse of last night. From the truck, Ben watched through the large plate-glass windows in the front of the store. One of the windows had a large crack running from one corner to the other, but it remained in place somehow.

Vince must have noticed him looking at the window. "Yeah, the shockwave broke a lot of windows. I have a few out back that I had to board up completely. I figure they must have hit Indianapolis by the direction of the flash. The shockwave hit us within a couple minutes of the blast."

"Joel and I were in the mountains at about 12,000 feet. It was quite the show from where we were. I've never seen anything like it before in my life, and I hope I never do again." Ben sighed.

"I can imagine." Vince raised an eyebrow.

"I know. It's something we'll never forget," Ben added.

With Vince refusing to let Ben pump his own gas, he was free to open up the back of the truck and look around for some of the things he thought

Vince would be interested in. He pulled out the .243 rifle he'd taken from the guy in the Bronco and the box of ammo he'd found for it. As he drew the long, polished wood and steel rifle from its case, he saw Vince's eyes light up.

"A .243 short mag and a box of ammo," Ben stated.

Vince grinned. "Now you're talking my language! What were you interested in trading for?"

"For starters, I was looking at that sack of rice and the dog food, and I wanted to take another look around in the daylight to see what else you had that we might be able to use. But the rifle is for all your hospitality and fixing the truck. It's the only way I can come close to repaying you for everything you've done for us."

"You don't owe me anything for that. But I can't say we couldn't use another accurate rifle. We're a little light on those."

Ben had seen some of the weapons the people on the wall were carrying last night. Most of them were toting shotguns or handguns. He only saw a couple rifles in the group. They needed a nice scoped rifle more than he and the kids did. They had more than enough weapons and ammo for the three of them. Besides, he felt guilty about not being able to help them out more and this was the next best way to clear his conscience about it.

Ben set the box of bullets on the tailgate and slid the rifle back into its case. He leaned the gun on the rear tire near Vince. "Take it. It's yours. I've got a few other things to trade for the food and fuel," Ben said.

Vince finished pumping gas, but before he put the pump back in its cradle, he paused. "How 'bout your spare tanks?"

"Thanks, but they're full," Ben replied as he continued to dig around in the back of the truck.

Vince hung up the pump and picked up the rifle and the box of ammo on the tailgate.

"I'll see you inside." Vince headed off toward the store.

"I'm right behind you," Ben said.

Gunner strained his neck, looking over the back seat as he watched Ben dig through their gear and gather items. He placed them in the center of a towel, then grabbed the corners and made a makeshift bag out of it to carry everything.

Before he closed the truck up, he thought for a second and reached under the back seat. He pulled out the small crate with the coins in it and counted out 16 of the one-ounce silver pieces. He filled his front pockets with the coins and stuffed the crate back under the seat. He wasn't sure if he would need them all, but he was feeling generous for all the kindness that had been shown to them.

"Good boy! We'll be right back," Ben reassured Gunner as he slung the makeshift bag over his shoulder and closed the back of the truck. He wasn't sure what Joel and Allie would want from Vince's store, but he wanted to make sure he had plenty to offer in exchange for the things they wanted.

This might be the last chance they had to resupply before they got to Maryland.

· 12 ·

When Ben got inside the store, Vince was standing behind the counter and had the .243 out of its case again and was looking it over. Joel and Allie were wandering around among the shelves, and Allie was balancing a sizable pile of apples, potatoes, carrots, and onions in her arms. Joel had picked up the large sack of rice and was carrying it with him as they browsed.

Ben headed straight to the counter, where Vince was admiring his new gun and laid the towel down. As he peeled back the corners of the old towel, the major looked away from the rifle to see what he had. Ben organized the two small fuel-burning camp stoves and three of the Spyderco knives that he and Joel had salvaged from his store in Durango.

"Won't you guys need those?" Vince asked as he leaned the rifle against the back of the counter.

"No. These are extra. But we're going to need

more of those fuel cylinders you've got up there." Ben pointed to the shelves on the wall behind the counter. There sat a row of four small fuel canisters that would work with their camp stove.

"So you want to give me a couple stoves and take all my fuel, huh?" Vince chuckled.

Just then, Joel and Allie approached the counter and unloaded the contents of their arms.

"This will last us a long time," Allie said as she tried to contain the produce as it rolled around on the counter next to the large bag of rice.

Ben suddenly felt self-conscience and realized how much stuff they were asking for. He felt guilty about what they were offering in return—not to mention he still wanted the dog food and the stove fuel. He also didn't want to risk offending the major. He was a standup guy and a man of his word, both of which were a rare commodity these days. But that was why Ben had brought a little something extra with him from the truck.

He reached into both pockets of his pants and pulled out two handfuls of silver coins. He spread out 16 shiny one-ounce silver coins in a row across the towel. A pound of silver coins ought to sweeten the pot.

"For all this, the dog food, and the fuel," Ben offered.

Vince picked one of the coins up. Holding it up to his face, he inspected it closely.

"Very nice." He nodded. "You've got yourself a deal."

He reached behind him and pulled the fuel canisters down from the shelf. He then moved the two camp stoves and all but one of the knives to the shelf where the fuel had been. Keeping one of the knives for himself, he tucked it in his back pocket before scooping up the coins, loading them into a small box, and placing them out of sight behind the counter.

Allie took advantage of the empty towel and gathered the produce in the center of it. She grabbed it by the corners and hoisted the heavy load into her arms.

"I'll take these out to the truck," she said.

Joel grabbed the case of canned dog food and threw the rice on top. "I got this. Right behind you." He followed Allie toward the truck, leaving Ben and the major alone once more.

"Let me give you a hand with these." Vince grabbed two of the small fuel tanks off the counter as he came around the side.

Ben took the other two and started for the truck.

"Don't wait too long to tell her," Vince warned. "I know you're not looking forward to it, but she's got to know. I could have one of the girls here talk to her, if you'd rather."

Ben stopped as he was about to open the door. "No, I'll do it. It needs to come from me."

Vince nodded and the two continued out to the truck.

The kids had already loaded their things and were closing the tailgate when Ben and Vince got there. Gunner was worked up and pacing the rear bench seat in anticipation of the trip. He had now fogged up a good portion of the side window.

Ben placed his two tanks into the back of the Blazer and then took the other two from Vince and did the same. He'd reorganized the back of the truck later and square away the new supplies. Right now, he wanted to get on the road. This little town had been a godsend, but it was time to move on.

Vince followed him around to the driver's door as the kids loaded up from the other side. Allie got in the back with Gunner, who was very excited to see her and acted as though they had been gone for hours. Joel slid into the passenger's seat and slammed the door shut. Ben got in and rolled his window down before pulling the door closed.

"Thanks again! For everything." Ben extended his hand.

Vince took his hand and hung on to it for a second. "If you don't find what you're looking for out there, you're always welcome here. All of you." He leaned into the truck a little and made eye contact with Allie and then Joel.

"Thanks," Allie said.

"Yeah, thanks," said Joel.

Ben started the truck and Vince took a few steps back.

"Good luck, guys! Be safe." Vince waved as they crept out from under the shade of the covered gas pumps and into the morning sun. Ben nodded at the major as they pulled away.

There was a small gathering of people in the motel parking lot across the street. Mary, Cy, and Reese were among the group and waved at them as they drove away. Ben and the kids waved back and headed for the gate.

Ben slowed as he rolled through the already-open gate. The guy manning the entrance waved from the dump truck. Ben smiled as they passed. He was glad to see they were now using the dump truck to block the gate. After they had gone through, Ben watched in the rearview mirror as the big red truck backed up and closed off the opening.

Then Ben focused his attention on the road ahead, only glancing at the rearview mirror a few more times before Cloverdale and the wall of cars faded from view.

The realization that they were on their own again sunk in and was their reality once more. The feeling was bittersweet for Ben, who should have been in good spirits after everything the kind people of Cloverdale had done for them. They had gotten some rest, fixed the truck, eaten well, and resupplied their food, fuel, and water.

But his heart was heavy with the thought of confronting Allie with the bad news. He glanced at her in the mirror. She was petting Gunner and looking through one of her books. She looked about as happy and content as he'd seen her yet, and he really hated the fact that he was going to ruin that.

For several miles, Ben wrestled with the idea of when and how to tell her, and he almost convinced himself to wait and see what they found when they got closer to Pittsburgh. But he wanted this off his chest, and he wanted to be fair to Allie. He knew what he had to do.

It was time to tell Allie what he'd learned.

· 13 ·

Ben slowed the Blazer down and pulled over to the side of the road.

"What's going on?" Joel asked.

Gunner lifted his head from Allie's lap as the truck came to a stop.

"Is there something wrong with the truck?" Allie leaned forward.

"No. I need to talk to you guys about something." Ben shifted in his seat and twisted around to face Allie.

"What is it?" Allie swallowed.

"When I was talking to Vince last night, he told me that Pittsburgh was destroyed in the attacks." Ben looked at Joel, then back at Allie, who was already shaking her head.

"Wh… What do you mean? How does he know? I don't understand… Destroyed?"

"He has a ham radio that he's been able to contact other areas with. Communication has been limited, though, and he doesn't know details. But the word is that Pittsburgh was hit by a lower-altitude detonation. A few other cities have been hit pretty hard as well. Washington D.C. is one of them."

"Let me out!" Allie blurted and covered her mouth with her hand as if she was going to get sick.

Joel scrambled to unbuckle himself and get out of her way.

She flew over the front seat and out onto the ground, where she landed on all fours and threw up. Joel kneeled down next to her and rubbed his hand on her back.

Gunner hopped down from the truck and ran over to where she was on the ground. He stood back a couple feet and watched her, confused about what was going on but aware that something was wrong. His tail hung limply, and his head tilted to the side as she continued to get sick.

Ben got out and walked around to their side of the truck and stood on the grassy shoulder for a moment before reaching into the truck and retrieving Allie's water bottle and a towel. He handed the towel to Joel, who was still kneeling next to her.

Allie sat up and took the towel from Joel. She held it up to her face and remained that way for a minute. Gunner approached her now and pushed his snoot into the towel, trying repeatedly to engage Allie in some type of interaction.

"Gunner, easy," Joel said.

"It's okay," she mumbled through the towel, reaching out blindly with one of her hands. She wrapped her arm around Gunner's neck. Gunner sat down next to her, looking content now that she was touching him.

Ben felt like he should say something. "I still intend on going that way, Allie. We'll find out for ourselves what's going on in Pittsburgh. We're not giving up." Ben tried to sound hopeful but he didn't want to come off as patronizing. He knew the odds that her dad was all right were slim to none, and so did she.

Allie slowly lowered the towel to reveal red puffy eyes and a pale white face. She continued to stare off into the distance for a while longer without saying anything to either Joel or Ben.

She slowly stood and turned to face them. "We're wasting time here then." She almost choked on her own words and began to tear up again.

Joel quickly went to her side and put his arm around her. She leaned into him and sobbed loudly. Ben went over to where they were standing and hugged them both. She was trying to be tough and it was commendable, but even Ben found himself fighting off tears as his empathy for her overwhelmed him. He couldn't imagine how she felt now. Losing both parents was enough to destroy someone emotionally under normal circumstances. But on top of the struggles this new world presented, he wouldn't blame her or think any less of her if she had a full-blown meltdown right here and now.

After what must have been at least a minute of standing in their huddle of silence, except for the occasional sniffle or sigh, they all stepped back. Allie wiped at her eyes with the towel and looked at Joel, then Ben.

"I can't believe it's just me now. I'm all alone. There's no one left but me," Allie said with a blank look on her face.

Ben looked at her and put his hand on her shoulder until she made eye contact. "You're far from alone. We're here for you."

"You're part of this family now," Joel said as he wiped a tear from his eye. He looked at his dad and then at Allie as he said it. Ben nodded in agreement and handed Allie the water bottle. She took a mouthful and swished it around before turning away and spitting it out. Then she took a big drink of the cool water and wiped the sweat from her brow.

"I guess we better get going, huh?" Allie said softly.

"Come on, boy," Joel called Gunner to the edge of the truck, where he helped the big dog back into the vehicle.

Allie followed and began climbing into the back.

"Do you want to sit up front for a while?" Joel offered.

"No thanks. I'm good back here for now. Maybe later." Allie continued to the back seat, where Gunner was waiting for her.

Ben got settled behind the wheel and didn't waste any time. Before Joel had his door all the way closed, the Blazer started moving forward. Ben steered the truck back onto the interstate and accelerated quickly. He felt like the more distance they could put between them and where he had told Allie the news, the better they would feel.

But no amount of distance would lighten the mood or soften the blow she'd just been dealt. Ben knew there was nothing more to say right now and Allie would talk when she was ready.

They traveled on in near silence for the next couple hours. The only conversation concerned navigating the secondary roads around Indianapolis and getting back onto I-70 after they were safely past what remained of the large city. From what they could see, Indianapolis was a burned-out shell of its former self, not unlike most of the other places they'd passed. No one commented on anything as they drove.

They had all officially become numb and indifferent to the post-apocalyptic landscape that rolled by outside their windows. It was a sad truth to accept, but Ben knew it was inevitable.

· 14 ·

Not long after getting back on I-70, they passed a road sign that read COLUMBUS OHIO 160 MILES. Allie tried to ignore the rest of the sign, but she couldn't. The bright white letters that read PITTSBURGH 340 MILES seemed to jump out at her. It was stuck in her head now, and it hurt like a punch to the stomach.

She sipped on her water in an effort to calm down and fight off the nauseous feeling that welled up again in her throat. With a few deep breaths, she was able to keep the feeling at bay until it passed. She was going to have to come to terms with all of this and with whatever they found when they got close to Pittsburgh.

She kept trying to remind herself that she wasn't alone and that she had Joel and his dad and Gunner, and that was a lot. In fact, it was the only reason she was still alive.

But she still couldn't accept the fact that she was

the last survivor in her family. She wasn't under the illusion that life would ever really be the same again, but now there was a certainty to it. And it stung with a finality that she couldn't shake from her thoughts.

She wanted to know more about what had happened in Pittsburgh, but she didn't want to at the same time. Reluctant to start up a conversation about it, she kept silent.

Joel kept checking back on her occasionally, but she could barely manage a nod to let him know she was okay. There was nothing he could say to take away the things she was feeling right now. There was nothing anyone could say, really.

It was going to take time to heal from these wounds. She had allowed herself to have more hope in finding her dad than she should have. She kept telling herself that it might not work out and that there was a good chance they wouldn't even be able to find her dad. But in her heart, she'd believed they would.

Joel's dad would come through like he had with everything else and they would find him and everything would be okay. That was how it played out in her mind, anyway. It was the only thing that had kept her going at times during this journey. Now there was nothing—at least, that was how she felt. She knew it wasn't true, but she didn't care at the moment.

Everyone seemed content to ride in silence for now, and that was fine with her. Even Gunner was unusually calm and seemed uninterested in the passing landscape. It was plenty hot, but they were able to maintain enough speed to keep a steady flow of air moving through the truck. They only slowed down a handful of times to make their way around some obstacles on the road.

The news of Pittsburgh had somehow taken the shock value out of the burned-out buildings and wrecked cars. Allie found herself easily ignoring what had once drawn her attention. It wasn't that she didn't care about the lives that had been lost. It was more that she felt she didn't have the energy to care about it anymore. Or maybe they just paled in comparison to the wreck her own life had become.

Ben broke the silence "We'll be in Ohio in about half an hour or so. Making pretty good time today."

"How are we on gas?" Joel asked.

"Just under half a tank. We'll stop when we get off the interstate to go around Columbus, if we can hold out that long." Ben glanced around the truck.

"I'm good to keep going for a while," Allie answered.

"Good." Ben nodded and pulled the atlas out from between the seats and tossed it into Joel's lap. "Why don't you find us a good route around Columbus?"

"Did the major say anything else about Pittsburgh?" Allie met Ben's gaze in the rearview mirror.

"No, just that it had been hit pretty badly. Some of the detonations happened at lower altitudes in a few places across the country. Pittsburgh is believed to be one of those places," Ben answered.

"But what would happen? I mean, what would that do to a place?" she asked.

Ben sighed as his face tightened. "If these places were ground zero for a nuke, there might not be much of anything left within a six- to ten-mile radius. Depending on the payload, the shockwave could reach out for miles. I suspect we'll know the truth long before we get there."

Allie nodded and sat back against the seat.

Still half asleep, Gunner stretched his limbs and pushed his head up against her leg before closing his eyes once more.

Allie knew what it meant if Pittsburgh had taken a direct hit, but hearing it from Ben made it real. She was at least thankful for his honesty, and it meant a lot to her that he wasn't trying to downplay the reality of the situation.

She made up her mind. If they got close to Pittsburgh and saw that it was hopeless, she would insist on not wasting any more time there and that they continue on to Maryland. They had sacrificed so much for her already. It was time to face reality and stop penalizing Joel and his dad for her misfortune.

They had gone above and beyond to help her, and she would do everything in her power to help them get to Bradley and Emma before it was too late.

· 15 ·

Ben now saw that his original plan, to get off the interstate long before Indianapolis and head north, was a huge waste of time and unnecessary. If Pittsburgh really was as bad as Vince said, there was no need to waste valuable time on a northern route around Indianapolis and Columbus. The interstate would take them to within 30 or 40 miles of Pittsburgh. If it was in fact ground zero for a nuclear detonation, that would be plenty close to make an assessment of the chances for survivors.

Ben was relieved that they could stay on or near I-70. It meant getting to his kids at least a day sooner. He would have been downright happy about it if it hadn't come at such a high cost to Allie. He wasn't exactly thrilled at the thought of a late-night insertion into Pittsburgh to grab her dad, but he certainly hadn't wanted it to go down like this.

He thought she'd handled it pretty well considering she'd lost both parents in little more than a week's time. Ben glanced at her in the rearview mirror. She had fallen asleep with Gunner in her lap. The poor girl needed the rest. The emotional strain she was under would crush a lesser person. And they hadn't really gotten the sleep he was hoping for last night, thanks to the late-night raid on Cloverdale.

It had been nice to sleep in a bed for a change, though, however brief, and his back was feeling better for it. There would be no such luxury tonight, however. It was back to tents and sleeping bags on the ground wherever they ended up today.

"Dad, do you think they're okay?" Joel said quietly. "Mom and them, I mean. You said that D.C. was hit pretty bad."

"They're a good four hours from D.C. It shouldn't have affected them there. I'm more concerned with getting around D.C. and Baltimore right now. If your mom got them to Grandpa Jack's, they should be fine."

Joel nodded and focused his attention back out the window, apparently satisfied with his answer.

Ben's real concern was how close the kids were to Norfolk, Virginia. They were just across the Chesapeake Bay, really only a couple hours from the naval base there, as the crow flew. The major hadn't mentioned Norfolk, but Ben found it hard to believe the North Koreans wouldn't take a shot at the largest navy base in the U.S.

Joel turned back to face Ben, then looked at Allie. "What about Pittsburgh? Do you really think it's that bad?" he whispered.

Ben looked at Joel briefly. "Yeah, I do. I mean look at the places we've been through. There's nothing left of most of them, and if Pittsburgh did take a direct hit, there won't be anything left of it, either."

Ben checked on Allie to make sure she was still sleeping. "We'll see for ourselves soon. The interstate will take us close enough to know if they were hit or not."

"Look!" Joel pointed to what remained of the Indianapolis International Airport on their left.

Ben inspected the once-busy airport, reduced now to a graveyard of dead aircraft and burnt rubble. Some of the planes still sat at their gates, waiting for passengers that would never come. Luggage was scattered all over the ground, around some of the service vehicles, and underneath the intact planes.

Most of the suitcases and bags were open, their contents strewn all over the ground. Ben wondered if that was the result of looters or an accident.

There were very few intact planes, and most had been reduced to wreckage on the runway. A few planes that Ben assumed were in the process of landing or taking off had fallen from the sky and landed on the main terminal. Several tail sections stuck out of the terminal roof as if they had been stuck there like darts into a dartboard.

The building still smoked in certain areas, even after more than a week since the attacks, no doubt from the jet fuel. Some parts of the building had resisted the flames but had melted instead. It was hard to take in the amount of destruction that had happened here, and the whole thing looked surreal and fake. But it wasn't. It was very real, and the burning odor that stung at his nose and throat was proof.

"Oh man, that stinks." Joel made a face and covered his nose.

A smell that reminded Ben of burnt rubber permeated the air. He was happy to see the exit for the 465 expressway around the city on his right. He eagerly steered the Blazer onto the exit ramp and away from the interstate and the devastated airport.

He was glad Allie was asleep and had missed that. There was a good chance her mother had been involved in a scene like that. Whatever airport her mother had been unlucky enough to be at when the bombs had gone off probably looked similar.

They all probably did. With dozens of outgoing and incoming flights suddenly left dead stick, the result could be nothing less than catastrophic. Ben thought for a moment about what must have been a staggering number of lives lost at the nation's airports alone—not to mention the thousands of other planes that had gone down mid-route like the one he and Joel had witnessed in the mountains.

"Keep a lookout for a good place to get gas, although I wouldn't mind getting away from this smell and smoke first." Ben was anxious to turn his thoughts away from what they had just seen.

"I'm looking." Joel's voice was muffled through his T-shirt, which he had pulled over his mouth and nose.

Gunner popped up in the rearview mirror as he sat up from his sprawled-out position across the rear bench seat and Allie's lap. He stuck his head toward Ben's open window, between the seat and the truck, and sniffed the air. Letting out a big yawn, Gunner finished with a whimper and shuffled impatiently on and off his bad leg.

"We better stop sooner rather than later. I think Gunner needs to go." Joel looked back at the dog, who was now leaning heavily on Allie.

Ben watched in the mirror as Allie slowly came to and rubbed her face. He was hoping the short nap would boost her spirits a little, although he didn't expect her to have moved on from the bad news by any stretch yet. He was disappointed to see that she still had that same blank look on her face as she stared out the window. She was pale and looked how he imagined she probably felt.

"We're stopping soon. We can get out and stretch our legs for a bit." Joel glanced at her.

She just nodded.

"We're making pretty good time. Maybe we can take a break and fix something to eat if we can find a good spot to stop. A few more miles and we can get off the expressway and back onto the interstate," Ben said.

She shrugged. "I'm not really that hungry."

"You need to eat. You have to keep your strength up, and it will help you feel better," Ben said.

"I know," she admitted. "I just don't really have an appetite."

"I'm sure you don't, but we need you, Allie. We need you here with us," Ben said.

They drove on in silence for several more miles until they picked up I-70 once more on the other side of Indianapolis. As the remains of the city shrunk in the rearview mirror, the landscape quickly returned to a more rural setting.

Ben spotted a tall yellow and red Pilot Flying J travel center sign a mile or so up ahead. The gas station sat off the interstate a few hundred yards on a secondary road. A few other buildings were visible farther down. Across the street from the service station was an old white church building with a post office next door.

The area looked innocent enough, and Ben was

satisfied that it was a suitable spot to take a break and get some fuel. After doing the customary lap around the place, it checked out okay and they parked by the fuel tanks.

Gunner was anxious to get out and nearly climbed over Joel getting out of the truck.

"Easy, boy. Hang on a second!" Joel hopped out of the way as the dog bounded by him, not seeming to be bothered by his injury at the moment.

Gunner raced over to an old trash can and relieved himself right away.

Allie made her way out of the truck slowly and began to gather the things they would need to make lunch.

Ben got out of the truck and brought the AR with him. He laid it across the hood and stretched his back. He then rolled his neck from side to side, making a loud cracking sound.

Allie stopped rummaging in the back of the Blazer and looked at him. "You okay to drive? That didn't sound too good."

"Oh, those are normal sounds after 40. It actually felt pretty good," Ben joked as he joined Joel in getting the fuel pump and hose set up.

Allie shook her head and cracked a small smile before she let her hair fall over her face and resumed gathering lunch supplies.

Ben was glad to see a little bit of life in the girl. "How about we use some of the fresh produce?"

"Okay," she said without looking up.

He was worried about her and for good reason. He had seen many people lose the will to fight in the face of adversity and tragedy. It was a slippery slope and a hard one to come back from once the feeling of defeat or hopelessness took hold.

As a unit, they couldn't afford that now, though. They couldn't let her slip into that mindset.

There was a fine line between giving her space to grieve and making sure she knew they were there for her, and Ben was doing his best not to cross it.

· 16 ·

Ben and Joel made quick work of the fueling and Ben kept an eye out for trouble during most of the process while Joel ran the pump.

Allie joined Gunner near a large oak tree a safe distance from the refueling and was working on lunch over the stove. Gunner found a stick to chew on and was content to lay in the shade with it near Allie. Joel pulled the truck under the tree and into the shade once the pump and hose were put away. Ben took the AR and walked over to where Allie was preparing lunch for them.

"That looks good," Ben said.

"Just rice, carrots, and onions with a little salt and pepper, but at least it's something different." Allie sighed.

"Well, it smells good and I'm hungry," Joel chimed in as he opened one of the cans of dog food for Gunner and shook the contents into a bowl with a plop.

The sound was enough to lure Gunner away from Allie. He got up and made his way over to the collapsible orange bowl and devoured the food within minutes.

They sat around under the shade of the tree and ate their lunch. Not much was said as they ate. The shade provided some relief from the midday heat, but Ben was anxious to get back on the road. With any luck, they could make the Pennsylvania border before they stopped for the night.

Ben also knew there was a chance that they'd be close enough to Pittsburgh tonight to see the damage firsthand. Or at least they would start to see signs if it was in fact ground zero. Another couple hours and he imagined the landscape would begin to show the effects of a nuclear explosion. It would be tough for Allie, but she would have to deal with it, regardless of what they found.

As they cleaned up from lunch and stowed things back in the Blazer, Gunner picked up the trail of something interesting and slowly followed it toward a dumpster in the corner of the service station lot.

"Joel, how about driving for a while?" Ben asked.

"Okay, no problem." Joel made his way around the front of the truck and noticed Gunner now sniffing around the old rusty dumpster.

"Come on, boy. Let's go."

Gunner ignored Joel and continued his search.

"Gunner, let's go!" Joel raised his voice.

Ben and Allie had stopped now and were waiting with the passenger door open for Gunner to come back and load up in the truck.

Just then they heard a noise from inside the dumpster. A few seconds later, a startled raccoon popped its head out of a hole in the bottom corner of the dumpster where the metal had rusted through.

Ben knew what was going to happen next, and there was nothing he could do to stop it.

"Gunner! No," Ben yelled.

But it was too late. The two animals had seen each other and the game was on. The raccoon swiftly pulled the rest of itself out of the hole in the dumpster and took off running. Gunner hesitated briefly but gave in to his instincts and darted after the scared animal. The raccoon headed for the church across the street.

"Get the truck and meet me over there." Ben ran after Gunner, leaving Joel and Allie at the truck.

They quickly loaded up, and Ben heard the Blazer start up as he chased after the dog. Gunner's leg was either feeling fine or he was so worked up at the sight of the critter that he had forgotten about it. Ben was unable to catch them, and the raccoon ran up the steps to the church and went inside through the partially open front door.

Gunner paused on the front stoop of the old building and sniffed around for a second.

"Gunner!" Ben shouted again, but it was in vain. Gunner looked back at Ben as he approached and Ben realized that he intended to end his little game of tag.

The dog forced his way between the double doors and disappeared into the building.

"No!" Ben sighed. The Blazer slid to a stop behind him in the gravel parking lot of the church. He turned around as Allie and Joel jumped out of the truck.

"Gunner went in," Ben huffed as he tried to catch his breath.

"I know. We saw him go in," Joel said as he and Allie started up the church steps.

Ben was about to tell them to wait when they heard a scream come from inside the building, followed by a few barks and growls from Gunner.

"Wait! You can't just go in there." Ben pulled out his pistol and stepped in front of the kids when he caught up to them on the stoop.

"Nice and easy," Ben said.

Joel and Allie followed his lead and got their pistols out as well.

Ben looked through the partially opened door, but it was too dark to see anything. The thick stained-glass windows had somehow survived the shockwave and were filtering out what little sunlight penetrated the interior of the church.

The light there was came through in the colors of the glass and served only to highlight the dust particles floating in the air. He squinted as he tried to see inside and look past the colored light. Leading the way with his pistol at the ready, he opened the door slowly and made his way in.

Joel and Allie were right behind him.

The church was small and only had a couple dozen wooden pews. A red-carpeted aisle ran down the center of the sanctuary and led to a small pulpit on an elevated stage.

Once they were inside, Ben's eyes began to adjust and he could see Gunner in a defensive stance at the front of the church, growling.

He had a young couple with a small child backed into a corner. The man was holding a chair up, the legs pointing out in an effort to keep the dog at bay. The woman was hunched behind him with a young boy in her arms.

From what Ben could tell, they looked unarmed, other than the chair. He figured if they had any other weapons, they would have used them by now.

As he got closer, he could see more of what was going on and realized they posed no threat to him and the kids. The man was struggling to hold the chair up as it was.

Their faces were thin and pale, and the desperation in their eyes was painfully obvious. His concerns quickly faded when he realized the severity of their condition. These people weren't dangerous. They were dying.

· 17 ·

"Gunner, heel up," Ben commanded sternly.

Gunner relaxed his stance and backed up a few steps before sitting down. Ben took a couple steps forward to meet the dog while he tucked his pistol away and grabbed Gunner's collar. He felt bad about Gunner cornering them and wanted to assure them that the dog was no longer a threat.

The man let the chair fall to the carpeted floor with a thud.

"Sorry about that," Joel apologized. Holstering his gun, he kneeled next to Gunner and held his collar, taking over for his dad. "He got a little wound up chasing that raccoon."

Allie followed suit and put her gun away as well. "Are you okay?"

The man nodded "We… We were just getting water," he mumbled weakly. Leaning on the chair, he pointed to the baptismal tank at the rear of the stage area behind the pulpit.

The little boy, who couldn't have been more than five or six, turned his head to look at them, mostly focusing on Gunner, before burying his face back in the woman's neck.

"Where are you from?" Ben asked.

The man mustered a little more energy for his response this time, but his voice was still weak. "We live down the road. We just come here for water."

Ben stepped up onto the stage and walked over to the baptismal tank to inspect it. The water had a greenish tint and there was a heavy film of dust lying on the still surface.

"I hope you're boiling this before you use it for anything," Ben warned.

By the looks of the ragtag couple and child, he guessed they weren't. The man shrugged but didn't say anything.

He looked like he was having a hard time staying upright as he continued to use the chair to prop himself up. The woman leaned against the wall and finally set the boy down. Barely able to stand, she found the closest pew and sat down with a sigh. The boy followed her over and sat beside her, immediately tucking himself behind her arm as best as he could.

"He's friendly once he gets to know you," Joel said. Gunner had settled down now and was more interested in finding the raccoon than interacting with the strangers. Joel released his grip on Gunner's collar and let him loose to explore.

The boy pulled closer to his mother when Gunner came their way but relaxed a little when the dog continued past them with nothing more than a look in their direction. Gunner had picked up a scent trail and was focused on resuming his pursuit of the raccoon.

"Hi, I'm Allie. What's your name?" Allie kneeled down to the boy's level, but he shied away and pulled in tighter to his mother again and tried to hide his face.

The mother spoke for him. "His name is Danny."

"Hi, Danny. I'm Allie. Nice to meet you." Allie tilted her head and leaned in to look at something Danny had pinned to his shirt. The boy peeked out from behind his mother's arm as Allie inched closer.

"That's really cool! Where did you get that?" Allie reached out and touched the shiny gold-colored wings pinned to the boy's shirt.

Again, he remained silent, forcing the mother to speak for him. "A few days ago, I think. I've lost track now. Some people came through and stopped here overnight. One of the women in the group gave him the wings."

Allie turned to look at Joel, then Ben. Her eyes were red and watery, but she also had a look on her face that Ben hadn't seen in a while.

"What is it?" Joel asked. Ben came down off the stage toward the kids and stood next to Allie.

"That's the airline my mom works for!" Allie turned back toward the mother. "Did you get the woman's name by any chance?"

"No, but there were five of them. They spent the night here before heading out on foot. One of the men with them said they were headed east." She struggled to hold the boy, who had climbed into her lap while trying to keep an eye on Gunner in the back of the church.

"What did she look like?" Allie pressed her for more information.

"About your height and blonde," the woman replied.

Just then, it dawned on Ben that the Blazer was open and exposed out in the parking lot.

"Joel, is the truck open?" Ben glanced at Joel, who immediately knew what he was getting at.

"I'll check on it," Joel answered. But before he left, Ben grabbed his shoulder and leaned in close. "Grab a couple MREs, will you?" he whispered.

Joel nodded and headed toward the door.

"Did they say where they were going, other than east?" Allie asked the woman and then glanced at the man, desperate for information.

"No. We were coming to get water and met them as they were leaving. They said they had come from Indianapolis, where they were forced to crash-land their plane. One of the men with them was hurt from the crash and his shirt was covered in dried blood. I think they were all part of the crew," the man said while breathing heavily. He made his way around to the front of the chair he was using as a shield and sat down with a groan.

Gunner had given up his search for the elusive raccoon and joined Allie near the woman and child. He sniffed at the two of them sitting on the pew as the little boy tried his best to stay out of reach.

"It's okay. He won't hurt you." Allie rubbed Gunner's head and told him to sit down. Gunner planted himself with a grunt and focused his attention on the man leaning over in the chair.

Ben had seen enough and heard enough to know that these people weren't going to last long. If they had been drinking this water without boiling it first, there was no telling how long they would survive without medical help. He also knew there was nothing he could do for them. As cruel and uncaring as it seemed, he had to leave them to their fate. The young boy reminded him of Bradley, though, and he couldn't walk away without giving them something.

The MREs wouldn't change anything, but he hoped it would ease their suffering for at least a little while. He also hoped it would diminish the guilt building up inside of him over their situation and help clear his conscience.

Joel hurried back in from the parking lot, carrying a couple green bags tucked under his left arm. "Here you go." He handed the MREs to Ben.

"I'm sorry. This is all we can spare." Ben apologized and set the meals on the pew next to the woman. "If you have the means to boil your water, you really should do that before you use it for anything," he warned again.

"Thank you," the woman said softly as she pulled the pouches close to her.

"Thank you for the information," Allie replied.

"Good luck." Ben felt awkward and a little foolish as he began to back away. No amount of luck was going to save them. Thanks to the water they had been drinking, their fates were sealed. He gave them a few days at best.

Gunner and the kids followed him after saying goodbye to the people and they all made their way out into the bright afternoon sun.

"Still want me to drive?" Joel asked.

"Sure, it's all yours," Ben said.

As they loaded into the truck and pulled out, Ben noticed Allie's silence and knew her mind was working over the possibilities of what she had just been told. He knew her well enough by now to expect at least a small argument about doing more for the people in the church—or at the very least a plea to leave them with more food. But she was preoccupied with the new information, and he could tell.

He was glad to see a change in her demeanor, but he was afraid it would only lead to more disappointment down the road. The roller-coaster of emotions was taking its toll, and he didn't want to see her spirit crushed yet again when things didn't pan out.

· 18 ·

As they pulled out of the church parking lot, the image of the family burned into Ben's mind. He couldn't help but wonder how much longer they would last. They watched him and the kids leave like their last chance for salvation was walking out the door.

But what choice did Ben have? He and the kids couldn't afford to part with any more food. He probably shouldn't have given them the MREs as it was, but he didn't regret doing it.

Ben wasn't used to being selfish when it came to looking out for people's welfare, and it was something he was going to have to learn to get over if he and the kids were to survive. This was the way things were now, and they couldn't help everyone they met.

"They looked pretty rough, huh?" Joel asked.

"Yeah, I feel bad for them, but what could we do? We're barely getting by ourselves," Allie answered.

"They've been drinking the water out of that old baptismal tank in the church without boiling it! Nothing we can really do for them. The MREs might buy them a little time, but that's about it," Ben added.

He was surprised to hear Allie's response, but she was mostly right, although he liked to think they were doing a little better than getting by. At least they were better off than most of the people they had run into, with the exception of the folks in Cloverdale.

"What do you think about what they said? I mean, it could be my mom. She flies through Indianapolis all the time. I've heard her mention it. She told me she had a super-early flight that morning for some type of training. Maybe they made it before the bombs." Allie unloaded with a slew of thoughts.

Ben knew it was coming and was prepared.

"It's probably a long shot, but anything's possible. If they're headed east on I-70, we should run into them sooner or later. It shouldn't be too hard to spot a group on foot." Ben was trying to be optimistic with a heavy dose of reality mixed in.

He knew the chances of finding her mother out here were slim to none. She worked for one of the major airlines with thousands of other employees. The chance it was Allie's mother who gave the boy the wings was even slimmer.

But at least it was something else for her to focus on other than the grim likelihood that Pittsburgh had been destroyed and her father was dead.

"We'll keep a look out, that's for sure. It could be her. You never know." Joel glanced back at Allie, who was already looking out the window and intently focused on their surroundings and maybe the possibility of seeing her mother again.

"Look! Ohio." Joel pointed.

Ben glanced up from the map. "Excellent. We're making good time. We should make the Pennsylvania border without any trouble before we stop for the night. Maybe even farther."

Now that they had crossed into Ohio, Ben knew they'd be approaching Columbus within the hour, if all went well. Then, just a few hours more and they'd have their answer about Pittsburgh firsthand.

But right now, they needed to focus on finding a suitable route around Columbus. Although I-70 pretty much ran straight through the city and it was tempting to press on and use the relatively easy-to-travel interstate, he knew it wasn't a good idea.

"We're looking for 270. It makes a tight loop around the outskirts of Columbus. I think that's the way we want to go unless things change as we get closer." Ben scanned the road ahead before turning to look at Allie.

"How are you holding up back there?" he asked.

"Okay," she answered without looking away from the window.

He could tell she was fully invested in the possibility that her mother was out there. They hadn't seen anyone on the road since they left the church, and Ben wasn't optimistic about their chances of finding the small group that the woman mentioned. And with each passing mile, the chances dwindled.

The woman at the church said they left a few days ago. Ben figured they might be able to walk 15 miles a day, and that was probably a generous estimate. In this heat and with limited supplies and water, the travelers wouldn't have gotten very far.

Ben thought back to the short distance they had traveled on foot when the Blazer broke down and how difficult that was. They had most likely passed the distance the group could have traveled a while ago. But he wasn't about to tell Allie that.

The only way they could have gotten any farther than this would be if they had hitched a ride with someone or found a running vehicle and commandeered it—both of which he thought were unlikely, although the more he thought about it, the less he discounted that possibility. After all, he and Joel had hitched a ride with Dale in Durango and then they had all gotten a ride from the major, so maybe it was possible.

He had to constantly remind himself that there were decent people out there and not everyone had nefarious intentions.

The other thought that crossed his mind was the possibility that they might not travel during the heat of the day. If he and the kids were on foot, they would certainly avoid traveling at this time of day. The group could have very easily taken shelter somewhere and waited for cooler temperatures.

He wanted to remain hopeful for Allie's sake, but with each passing mile, it seemed more and more unlikely that they would find the group from the church. Even though Allie hadn't given up watching for them, he wondered if she had come to the same conclusion he had. She was a smart girl, after all, and had to know the odds of finding them weren't good.

"There it is: 270. Twelve miles ahead." Joel read the sign as they passed, leaving out the rest of the information listed below, which read COLUMBUS 20 MILES and, below that, PITTSBURGH 197 MILES.

They continued on in silence as they drove along the interstate. The only activity in the truck was Gunner. He was restless and continually shifted positions from lying down to wedging himself between the driver's seat and the truck to take advantage of the air flowing in the open window.

Joel scratched Gunner's head every time he pushed his head up alongside his seat toward the window until eventually he settled in and stayed put for a bit. It didn't last for long, though, and he sat up again when Joel slowed down and prepared to take the exit.

Halfway through the exit ramp, Joel was forced to slow down even more in order to avoid an 18-wheeler that had taken out a few cars along with an overhead highway sign.

The sign, now toppled from its base, lay across the road, blocking the ramp entirely. Joel cautiously drove around the accident, through the overgrown grass and weeds in the median. The vegetation smacked against the undercarriage of the truck. With no mower crews to keep the grass in check, nature was reclaiming the roadways at a steady rate.

Ben wondered how long it would be before the roads themselves started to give way and fall apart. As it was, some of the weeds had grown to within inches of the road signs they passed. In another couple of weeks, most of them would be unreadable due to the overgrowth.

That would add a whole new challenge to the trip and make it extremely difficult to navigate. And give them even more reason to get to Maryland and get back home as soon as they could.

· 19 ·

As Ben expected, the expressway around Columbus was littered with cars and trucks. They were frozen in the moment of the attack, on their way to work or making early-morning deliveries. The number of wrecks on the highway made him wonder if all the bombs had hit at the same time or if there had been a delay between locations. Passage here was slow-going and reminded him of some earlier sections of road they had traveled.

The difference now was that the wrecks weren't smoking anymore and the bodies were heavily decayed.

They were forced to pass by some of the gruesome scenes at a painfully slow pace, thanks to the congested road. That crawl allowed the smell of death and decay to occasionally creep into the truck as they drove through the chaos.

Joel eventually gave up on trying to use the road altogether and resorted to driving along the shoulder and through the tall grass.

"Try to use the road when you can. There might be parts or debris in the grass we can't see," Ben warned.

"Okay, but it's really bad through here," Joel answered.

"I know. Just take your time. Nice and easy." Ben could tell Joel was nervous and a little stressed out. He didn't blame him; this was the worst they'd seen it in a while.

It took them almost an hour to get around the city using 270, but eventually they saw a sign to rejoin I-70 a few miles ahead.

"I'm ready to get off this road," Joel said.

"Hang in there. Not much farther. I can drive for a while after this if you want," Ben offered.

"I'll be fine once we get back on the interstate. Hopefully it goes back to the way it was."

As soon as they took the exit to I-70, the abandoned vehicles and wrecks started to thin out. Leaving the congested expressway behind them, Joel was able to slowly resume traveling at a speed they were more accustomed to. Air began to flow through the open windows once again, providing much-needed relief from the heat.

Allie poured some of her water into a bowl and set it on the console. Gunner stopped his heavy panting just long enough to take a drink and resumed as soon as he was done.

"We're going to need to get water soon. We're really low," Allie said as she held up a nearly empty Nalgene bottle.

They had gone through a lot of water today. The long, hot drive around the expressway hadn't helped their situation any. Ben looked at the map and saw that they were approaching Buckeye Lake State Park a few miles ahead.

"Looks like we cross over a small river or stream up ahead that feeds into this lake. Keep your eye out for a good spot to stop." Ben held the map so Joel and Allie could see it.

The first water crossing they came to was nothing more than an irrigation ditch. There was no access to the water from the road where the interstate crossed the ditch, but Joel slowed the truck down anyway and pulled over to the shoulder. Ben leaned out of his window and looked over the concrete guardrail to the water below.

The water was dark brown and looked heavy with silt. But that wasn't the worst part. A rainbow of colors gleamed on the surface as they reflected the bright sunlight. The oily sheen ran as far downstream as he could see. For a brief moment, he thought he could even smell it.

He couldn't tell if it was oil or fuel, but it really didn't matter. Their water filter was good, but it wouldn't remove petroleum-based pollutants. It was only meant to remove dangerous bacteria and protozoa. This was much worse than what he'd seen at the plane wreck on their hike out of the mountains. That was only a small amount of hydraulic fluid. This was thick and covered the surface entirely.

"Not good. There's something in the water." Ben shook his head. "Oil or gas coming from upstream, maybe a car, maybe something larger. There's a lot of it in the water." Ben pulled his head back in the window and tried to look up the ditch past Joel.

"Maybe a car went off the bridge. Is there anything on your side?" Ben asked. If that was the case, then they could simply filter their water from above the accident.

"I can't see anything." Allie strained to see from the back window over the painted section of glass. Joel put the truck in park and got out. He jogged over to the other side of the bridge and looked over the edge.

"Nothing in the water over here, but I can see the oil slick. It must be coming from farther up," he reported.

"Ew, I can smell it now." Allie was leaning up over the driver's seat to get a better view.

"I wonder if it's coming from the city. There's a lot of it! The water looks thick." Joel hurried back to the truck and got in. "What a mess," he muttered.

"Who knows what happened? Either way, we're not getting any water from here," Ben said.

Not wasting any time, Joel put the still-running Blazer in gear and pulled out onto the road.

Ben wasn't surprised at the polluted water. He'd expected to run into this problem sooner or later. He just wished they were better prepared. Passing up the water at the church seemed like a missed opportunity now. It might have been dirty, but at least they could have filtered it.

"How much water do we have, Allie?" Ben asked.

She held up a Nalgene bottle and swirled the contents around inside. There was less than half the bottle. "That's it."

They were going to need more than that to carry them through the rest of the day, especially in this heat.

"Does that mean the whole lake is bad?" Allie asked.

"It depends on the size of the spill and how far upstream it happened. But I think we need to look elsewhere to be safe. It's not worth the risk." Ben checked the map for another water source that wasn't linked to the lake or any of its tributaries.

According to the map, there were a couple more spots ahead where they would cross over water. With any luck, the oil or whatever it was would be isolated to that one ditch.

The next crossing was a little larger and looked more like a natural river than the man-made ditch they had crossed a few miles back. But it was just as disappointing. The water didn't seem as polluted here, but that was probably due to the faster current. The oily sheen was still visible in the slack water and along the banks.

The sludge-laden river made the water in the baptismal tank look clean by comparison, and once again, Ben regretted not taking advantage of the opportunity back at the church.

Whatever happened was far enough upstream to affect these two bodies of water that were miles apart. That also indicated that it was more than a leaky vehicle. This was a spill on a much larger scale. Maybe a derailed train carrying fuel or a refinery failure somewhere was responsible. It was hard to say what had caused this mess.

But one thing was certain: they were going to have to move well beyond this watershed to find a source of drinkable water.

"Just keep driving." Ben sighed and pulled a pen out from the spiral of wire that made up the map's binding.

NO WATER, he wrote boldly on the map, marking the area they were currently driving through. They would have to plan ahead on their return trip to Colorado and make sure they had plenty of water on-hand before they got here. Or maybe they would avoid this area altogether and take a different route. There would be more of them and it would be later in the summer, which meant it would be even hotter than it was now.

Without anyone to clean this up or at least contain the spill, this area would be a dead zone for years to come.

· 20 ·

The kids' morale had already taken a blow today when Ben told Allie and Joel what he had learned from Vince about Pittsburgh.

But now the heat was starting to get to them, adding insult to injury. Without water to quench their thirst and cool them down, there was no relief. The air coming in the windows was hot and did little to help. According to the map, their next chance for water was well over an hour away. The streams and creeks they encountered in this area were all polluted.

Ben continued to search the map for a possible water source, but he was interrupted when Joel suddenly put the brakes on and brought the truck to a complete stop.

"What's going on?" Allie questioned as she held Gunner from sliding off the seat.

Joel pointed. "What's that?"

Ben pulled his M24 from under the back seat and positioned it out the window, using the side mirror as a rest. Using the scope, he scanned the camp and surrounding area. A mile or so off the exit sat a dozen or so white tents in an open field.

There were other temporary structures as well as a couple trailers and supply trucks. The whole encampment was surrounded by chain-link fence and was a few acres in size. A plywood watchtower stood near what looked like the main entrance to the camp. There was a Humvee parked to one side of the gate and a fortified checkpoint built out of sandbags on the right side of the entrance with two people guarding it.

"It's a FEMA camp!" Ben sighed and sat back in his seat.

Allie leaned forward between the front seats. "That's a good thing, right?"

"I'm not sure. It depends if they have supplies or if they've run out. It also depends on how they're running the place." Ben knew they needed water, and if they had supplies to give out, it might be worth a closer look. But the last thing he was going to do was drive their supply-loaded truck up to the front gate. If the camp was running low on provisions, the National Guard wouldn't hesitate for one second to confiscate their truck or their gear. He wasn't even sure if it was worth approaching the camp at all. But if FEMA did have food and water to give out, they would be foolish not to take advantage of that.

"Maybe the group from the church ended up there." Allie's voice was hopeful. Ben hated to admit it, but they could have.

"Only if they got a ride from someone. This is a long way to walk from the church," he answered.

"Well, what are we doing?" Joel asked.

Ben thought for a moment. "Drive up to that section of woods there and park in the shade while I think this through." Fortunately, there was a section of dense woods along the highway before the exit that led to the camp. They could hide the truck there and stay out of sight for now, at least until he could decide on a plan of action.

Allie wouldn't be satisfied unless they checked the place out, and he could understand that. The possibility that her only remaining family member could be at the FEMA camp was something she wouldn't be able to let go of—and for good reason. How could he deny her the chance to look for her mother?

Based on what they knew, Pittsburgh was off the table now, and they weren't going to have to spend a day or more looking for her father. He felt like this was the least he could do for her. How bad could it be? Searching the FEMA camp would be far easier than running the gauntlet of downtown Pittsburgh and trying to find her dad.

As Joel approached the wooded area, he slowed down and eased the Blazer off the road and through the tall grass and overgrowth until he found a spot that was hidden from both the road and the camp.

"This is good. Go ahead and shut it off." Ben opened his door and stepped out into the knee-high vegetation. Gunner stood up impatiently on the back seat, whining as he waited for an opportunity to squeeze out of the truck.

"Hang on, boy," Allie said as she got out behind Ben. But Gunner was too anxious and made his way out on Joel's side of the truck instead of waiting for her. Joel was barely out of the truck himself when Gunner hit the ground and took off through the tall grass.

"You'd never know his leg was injured." Joel shook his head as he walked around to the other side of the truck, where his dad and Allie were standing.

"So what's the plan?" Allie asked.

Ben could tell she was anxious to search the camp, and rightfully so, but they had to think this through.

"Joel, I want you to stay here with Gunner. Allie and I will walk to the camp from here." Ben took his pistol, still in the holster, from his belt and put it on the passenger's seat along with his pocket knife.

"We're going to get searched, so we need to leave everything here, Allie."

She nodded and took her pistol out as well and placed it on the seat next to his.

"Why do I have to stay here?" Joel asked.

"I need you to stay here and keep an eye on things, buddy. We're not going to be gone long. I don't want to spend any more time here than we have to. Besides, they won't let Gunner in," Ben answered.

"Well, at least we can keep in touch with the radio," Joel said.

Ben shook his head. "Nope. If I walk in there with a radio, they'll know someone else is out here. I also don't want them to confiscate it. We're going in there with nothing more than the clothes on our backs. I want you to set up in the woods—somewhere out of sight but somewhere you can see us approach the gate. We may need to get out of here in a hurry. If things go south, I'll give you a signal."

"Like what?"

Ben thought for a second. "How about I rub my neck like this?" Ben rubbed at the back of his neck as if he were trying to work out a kink. "You'll be able to see that easily if you use the scope on the M24."

Joel nodded. "Got it."

"If you see me doing that, assume the worst." Ben put his hand on Joel's shoulder. "You'll be all right. With any luck, we'll be back within the hour.

I still want to push for Pennsylvania today."

Ben recognized the look on Joel's face and knew he was disappointed at his role in this plan, but it was the smart thing to do. If it weren't for the possibility of finding Allie's mother, he'd suck it up and push on past the camp. It wouldn't be fun, but they'd make it to another water source.

They heard Gunner coming long before they could see him, the dense weeds giving away his location as they parted in his wake. Gunner finally emerged at their feet, panting heavily and covered in seeds and plant matter. He seemed pleased with himself and didn't waste any time putting his paws up on the sill of the open truck door. Looking back at Ben and the kids, he waited for a boost up.

"No, Gunner! We're staying here." Joel sighed. The dog slowly put his front feet back on the ground and sat down, uncertain of what was happening.

"Stay alert. We'll be back as soon as we can. I'm counting on you, Joel." Ben looked him in the eye and nodded before heading out.

Allie turned to follow him but stopped. Without saying a word, she stepped back toward Joel and gave him a hug. She turned away and quickly followed the trail Ben had started through the overgrown vegetation.

Gunner started along behind them until Joel called the dog back. Ben turned to watch a reluctant Gunner return to Joel at the truck. Joel already had the M24 over his shoulder and was locking up the Blazer.

Ben and Allie fought their way through the dense overgrowth and headed back to the road. They could have cut through the woods and taken a more direct route to the camp, but he didn't want to give away Joel's location.

Better to have the soldiers think they had come from the road, just to be on the safe side. He didn't like leaving Joel alone, but there was no telling what they would find once they got to the FEMA camp.

If martial law had been imposed, they would be at the mercy of the soldiers. This certainly wasn't the smartest thing he'd ever done. He just couldn't bring himself to say no to Allie. This was the only hope the poor girl had left.

The FEMA camp came into view as they passed the edge of the woods. They continued along the shoulder of the interstate until they reached the exit ramp. They were less than a mile from the front gate and out in the open. Ben was sure they had been spotted by now. He hated how exposed and defenseless he felt, but this was the way it had to be.

"Let me do most of the talking, okay? We need to give them as little information as we can. I think the best thing to do is play dumb." Ben remembered the name of the last town they recently passed.

"Okay."

"If they ask, we'll tell them we're from Pleasant Grove. It's a town we passed not too long ago. If they find out we're from Colorado, they'll know we didn't walk here," Ben said.

"Do you really think they would take the truck and our stuff?" Allie asked.

"I know they would. Running vehicles are in short supply. I have no doubt they're under orders to seize all assets. If they've imposed martial law, that means curfews and the suspension of civil law and civil rights for civilians," Ben answered.

"So basically, we have no rights." Allie frowned.

"I'm afraid so. And that's why the less they know, the better off we are." It dawned on Ben that he didn't know who they were looking for. After all this time together, he didn't even know Allie's last name.

"By the way, what's your mom's name?"

"Sandra. Sandra Young, but she goes by Sandy."

"I better know who I'm looking for in case they ask. I doubt the soldiers will know the names of the people there, but they should have a list. Depends how they're running things."

They were within a couple hundred yards of the gate now, and the two soldiers standing guard came out from under the shade of the watchtower to intercept them.

There was a soldier in the tower as well, who was checking them out through a pair of binoculars.

All three were carrying weapons. Ben heard a generator running in the background somewhere, beyond the trailers located at the front of the compound.

As he and Allie got closer, they passed a sign that was mounted to a four-by-four wooden post dug into the ground. Ben read the warning to himself as they passed.

THIS FACILITY HAS BEEN DECLARED A RESTRICTED AREA ACCORDING TO THE SECRETARY OF DEFENSE DIRECTIVE ISSUED UNDER THE PROVISION OF SEC. 21 INTERNAL SECURITY ACT. UNAUTHORIZED ENTRY IS PROHIBITED. ALL PERSONS AND VEHICLES ENTERING HEREIN ARE LIABLE TO SEARCH AND SEIZURE.

The last sentence on the sign was written in bold red letters.

USE OF DEADLY FORCE AUTHORIZED.

Allie must have read the sign as well, and she gave Ben a nervous look.

"It'll be okay. Just let me do the talking unless they ask you something directly. If they do, keep it short," he instructed.

· 21 ·

Ben made eye contact with the two soldiers as they approached and read their name tags.

The first to reach them was a woman with the name Ford on her ID tag, and Ben saw that she was the higher-ranking of the two, even though she was only a corporal. The lower-ranking private followed close behind. His last name was Price and he was a young man that couldn't have been long out of boot camp.

Ben noticed a few things right away that seemed a little off. Both of their uniforms were a mess, and the private's hair was a little long for Army regulations, especially for a boot. Ben was willing to chalk that up to the current state of affairs. With all that was going on, keeping up appearances probably wasn't a top concern.

He still couldn't help but think about the butt-chewing he would have received for looking like that when he was in. But the one thing that stood out the most to him and didn't add up, no matter how he tried to rationalize it, was the private's weapon. The corporal had a standard-issue M4, while the kid was carrying a civilian-style AR15 similar to Joel's but with a few obvious custom modifications.

The only reasoning Ben could come up with was the possibility that they were short of weapons and it had been confiscated for use. It still didn't sit right with him, though, and he was beginning to grow more suspicious by the minute.

"Hold there!" The corporal pointed to a spray-painted orange line on the ground several yards back from the chain-link gate. "Are you carrying any weapons?"

"No," Ben stated.

Without warning, the private approached and began to pat him down while the corporal gave Allie the same treatment.

"Arms up," the private ordered. Ben and Allie both complied and remained that way as they continued the search.

"What do we have here?" The woman stopped her hand over Allie's back pocket and fished out the small knife Ben had given her.

"I... I forgot that was in there. I swear." Allie apologized and looked at Ben sheepishly.

The corporal held the knife for a moment, and then, to Ben's surprise, she stuffed it into her own pocket. He was pretty sure that wasn't protocol.

"You in the Army?" the young private asked. He had obviously seen Ben's tattoos during the search.

"Yeah, got out a long time ago. Best day of my life was the day I got my DD-318," Ben quipped.

Allie shot him a confused look.

"Yeah, cool." The private grinned.

"Billy!" The corporal barked, clearly irritated at the kid. "Where are you guys coming from?"

"Pleasant Grove." Ben would have asked them if they had any food or water to give out, and he would have also asked if they had anyone there by the name of Sandra Young, but he knew it was pointless.

These weren't Army National Guard soldiers. They were imposters.

He slowly lowered his arms from the search and rubbed at his neck for a few seconds before returning them to his side.

Neither one of them had corrected him when he mentioned the DD-318. The certificate of release or discharge from active duty form was actually called a DD-214. It was common knowledge to anyone who had served or was currently serving, regardless of branch. And they would have called him out on that glaring mistake.

He'd known something was wrong from the moment they'd approached the camp. The place was undermanned. Other than these two and the one in the tower, he had only seen two other uniformed people walking around.

But before Ben could give it any more thought, Allie spoke up, unaware of the danger they were in.

"We're looking for my mom, Sandy Young. Do you have a list of the people here?"

Ben cringed as she spoke. She must have been so nervous that she failed to notice him signal Joel. Hopefully, Joel had seen it.

"No, we don't have a list, but you can look for yourself," the woman said.

"No, actually, we're okay. We should get going back home." Ben put his hand on Allie's shoulder and began to pull her backward.

But before he could take another step, the woman lowered her gun and trained it on them. "Oh no, I insist. Come on. This way," she demanded.

The kid had his rifle pointed at them as well now and motioned toward the gate with the tip of his gun.

Ben and Allie held their hands up and did as they were instructed. Joel would know now without a doubt that they were in trouble. As they were forced past the gated entrance, Ben mulled over their situation.

He couldn't believe he had allowed himself to get into this position. Had he listened to his gut, they would have avoided the place altogether. He also wondered what had happened to the real National Guard soldiers and FEMA workers that set up the camp. He wasn't sure what kind of game these fakers were playing here or what their angle was.

What purpose would they have with taking prisoners? Even if this group had overrun the original camp personnel, why would they stay? Why wouldn't they take whatever supplies were here and move on?

A lot of ideas and questions flashed through his mind as he tried to make some kind of sense of all this, but none of it really mattered.

What mattered now was finding a way out of here and getting back to Joel.

· 22 ·

As Ben and Allie were marched through the camp at gunpoint, Ben noticed signs of a gunfight. Some of the trailers they passed, as well as the tents, were riddled with bullet holes.

He also noticed one of the trailers had an air-conditioning unit on top that was running. The long PVC drain line that ran down to the ground from the roof dripped water onto the otherwise dry ground and made a small puddle. It only served as a reminder of how thirsty he was and added to his frustration.

Whoever was behind all this was most likely in that trailer. He tried to commit the camp layout to memory as much as possible while they weaved their way through the rows of white tents.

They emerged into a small clearing on the far side of the camp, where a lone tent was isolated from the rest of the compound by a chain-link fence and a locked gate.

The kid trying to pass himself off as a private ran ahead and unlocked the chain that ran through the gate. He swung the door open wide and waited for them to catch up.

"In there," the woman ordered.

Ben felt the rifle barrel in his back as she pushed him toward the opening. Allie was in front of him and entered first. He reluctantly followed her inside the enclosure and turned around to face their captors.

The gate slammed shut, and the woman kept the gun pointed at them until the kid got the chain passed through the mesh and locked in place. Without saying a word, the two imposters quickly turned and disappeared into the maze of tents through which they'd just come.

"Why would they do this?" Allie questioned. "Why?"

"They're not Army. I'm not sure what's going on, but I know that." Ben turned to look at the large white tent that was in their enclosed area.

"Who are they then?" Allie looked at him.

"I don't know, but we need to figure out how to get out of here." Ben wished that was his only worry, but he found himself equally concerned about what action Joel would take. Both kids had been through a lot, and they had both shown maturity beyond what Ben had hoped. But expecting Joel to get them out of this was asking too much.

He and Allie approached the oversized tent. It was large enough to fit several vehicles, but as they could see through an opening in the canvas, it was filled with cots on the ground.

They slowly entered the tent and got out of the afternoon sun, although it was just as hot, if not hotter, inside the tent. There was no air circulation and a musty smell filled the air. The tent was empty, but many of the cots had personal items on them or nearby on the floor. It was obvious that people were sleeping here, as more than a dozen of the cots were unmade and showed signs of use.

"Where is everybody?" Allie asked.

Just then, a diesel engine, like that of a large truck, roared to life. It sounded like it was coming from the road they came in on. It continued to get closer until it slowed to an idle and eventually went quiet.

Ben heard voices and doors being slammed. He jogged to the opening in the tent and looked out.

Allie followed, but he put his hand out and motioned for her to stay out of sight until he determined what was going on. She huddled behind him as he peered out of the doorway and watched as a line of people began to emerge from the tents.

They were walking the same route that he and Allie had been brought in on. Hunched over and broken, they slowly moved across the last open stretch toward the gate. Their clothes were ragged and stained with dirt and blood. Several of them had makeshift bandages fashioned out of torn strips of cloth. It was a mixture of women and men of varying ages. There were 18 of them in total.

Keeping them at gun point were the same woman and the kid that had brought Ben and Allie in. But with them now was a new guy in civilian clothes who was carrying an M4. He was helping the other two keep the captives in line and corral them toward the enclosure.

It was overkill, as most of the people shuffling along barely looked capable of walking on their own let alone making any escape attempts. Nonetheless, he kept his gun trained on the sad bunch until the last one was through the gate and it was locked.

One of the last stragglers in the gate, an older man with gray hair, turned and yelled back at the new guy, "What about our food and water?" His voice cracked.

"You're lucky you're getting anything at all after the way you worked today," the new guy scoffed before he turned and left back through the tents.

The two in uniforms followed him and left the ragged bunch without saying anything more. The ragtag group of prisoners now inside the gate began to disperse to different areas of the enclosure. Most of them headed for the tent where Ben and Allie had remained concealed.

Ben stepped back from the opening as the first man entered. Besides a blank look in their direction and a shake of his head, he hardly paid them any notice. The next man that came in had the same empty expression on his face.

"Welcome to hell," he muttered.

Ben stepped back and in front of Allie as the man passed by them and made way for the blonde woman behind him to enter the tent.

"Mom!" Allie screamed as she bolted past Ben and embraced the woman, nearly knocking her off her feet. Allie wrapped her arms around her mother, who hadn't even realized what was going on yet.

Ben saw the resemblance right away now that the two were standing next to each other. It took her mother a few moments before she managed a response.

"Allie? Is that you? I don't believe it." Her mother pushed her back away so she could get a look at Allie's face. She cupped her daughter's cheeks in her hands.

"It's me!" Allie sobbed and embraced her mother once more. This time her mother returned the affection, and the two stayed that way for a while before anything was said.

"I thought I might never see you again. How did

you get here? Where did you come from?" The questions started to flow as Allie's mother came to the realization that her daughter was standing in front of her. She grabbed her by the shoulders and looked at her again as if to make sure that it was really her.

"Mom, this is Ben Davis." Allie stepped aside and wiped the tears from her face, keeping one arm still around her mother's shoulder.

Ben nodded. "Nice to meet you. I wish it were under better circumstances."

"Me, too. I'm Sandy." She offered a weak hand, and as Ben took it, he saw how frail and tired she was.

"This is Joel's dad," Allie added. "Remember the boy I told you about from school?"

"Yes, but how did you find me? How did you end up here?" Sandy's eyes were filled with wonder as the others filed into the tent and sat down on their cots.

"It's a long story, but they found me at the house and I've been traveling with them since. They were taking me to Pittsburgh to find dad. I...I thought you were gone." Allie began to tear up as she spoke. Her mother pulled her in close.

Sandy looked at Ben through watery eyes. "Thank you for taking care of my daughter!"

"Sure thing. She's quite the trooper. We're lucky to have her with us."

Allie looked at her mom. "We ran into some people a while back at a church. There was a little boy with a pair of wings on his shirt. Was that you?"

Sandy shook her head in disbelief. "Yes, it was! But how did you know I was here?"

"We didn't," Allie said. "We took a chance, hoping you might have ended up here. What happened?"

"We were on an early-morning training flight to Indianapolis when the bombs went off. Fortunately, we were already making our approach before we lost power. Our pilot was able to bring us down safely, but we were lucky to make it out of the airport. Planes were falling out of the sky all around us. A few of us made it to the highway and started walking." Sandy paused for a moment. "I need to sit down."

Allie helped her over to one of the vacant cots and sat beside her. Ben took the cot across the narrow aisle from theirs and sat as well.

Sandy continued where she left off. "We knew we had to get out of the city. Things were starting to get really bad. I wanted to get back to you—to Durango—but I thought maybe I could get to your dad and then together we could make it back to you. We got a ride from an older couple in a pickup a day after we left the church, and they dropped us off here at this FEMA camp."

"What's going on here?" Ben asked.

"These people!" Sandy paused and looked out toward the compound. "They took the place over a couple days ago. Most of the troops got called away. We heard they were having problems at another camp outside of Cincinnati. After most of the soldiers left, they attacked the camp at night and took the place over. They've been holding us prisoner and forcing us to work for them."

"Work doing what?" Ben had an idea, but wanted to hear it for himself.

"During the day, they take us out in one of the big supply trucks and force us to scavenge and loot people's houses. They work us until we fill the truck with stuff and then they bring us back here."

"How many of them are there?" Ben asked.

"At least six that I know of." Sandy looked at the ground and let out a heavy sigh. "I'm the only one left out of our group. The others were killed the night they attacked the camp. We tried to help, but it was useless." She shook her head. "And now you're stuck here, too!"

Allie tried to comfort her mother and hugged her again. "We'll figure something out, right?" She looked at Ben. "I mean, Joel is still out there."

Ben glanced around at the others nearby, hoping they hadn't heard Allie mention Joel. "Let's keep that information to ourselves for now. We'll get out of here somehow. I just need to think."

For the time being, there was no reason to let anyone here know that they had a man on the outside. These people were in rough shape, and that bred desperation. He wasn't about to trust anyone in here with that information. He wouldn't put it past one of them to trade that knowledge to gain favor with their captors.

And if they were going to make it out of here alive, they would need every advantage they could get.

· 23 ·

As Ben sat quietly, thinking over their situation, he began to hear voices outside the tent.

Sandy picked her head up. "That's them, bringing food and water before they make us unload the truck." She grimaced. "At least that's how it's been working."

The voices grew louder until Ben heard the chain being unlocked and untangled from the gate. One of the guards shouted for everyone to stand back.

Ben, Allie, and her mom followed the others out of the tent slowly and watched from a distance as the younger kid named Billy pulled a cart with water and MREs into the enclosure. The woman and the man that had been there before stood guard, their guns at the ready, until Billy made his way back out and locked the gate.

"You got 15 minutes," the man in civilian clothes barked before the three of them disappeared through the tents once more.

The pathetic group of prisoners suddenly came to life with the promise of food and water as they descended on the cart. By the time Ben, Allie, and her mom got there, only one MRE remained. Fortunately, there were still several waters left behind.

"I'll share it with you guys." Sandy picked up the packet of food and a water bottle.

"No, you need it more than we do. I only want the water." Ben grabbed two of the plastic water bottles and handed one to Allie. He drank one down right away and then grabbed the last one on the cart before anyone else claimed it.

He couldn't help but think about Joel and Gunner out there as he sipped on the second bottle. He hoped Joel would drink the last of the water they had and stay hydrated. But he knew his son too well and was worried that he would end up sharing it with Gunner in spite of needing it for himself.

Poor Joel out there on his own, no doubt scared and worried about them. He wished there was some way he could communicate with him, even if it were just to let him know that they were at least okay. Ben knew he was going to have to come up with an idea fast or else Joel would attempt something on his own.

The thought of his son singlehandedly trying to take on all of these guys was more concerning to him than their immediate situation.

If they were going to be forced to unload the truck later, maybe an opportunity would present itself then? That was the only thing Ben could think of right now. Breaking out of this enclosure wasn't an option. The razor wire around the top of the fence guaranteed that.

Ben glanced around at the people he was stuck with. He thought about talking to a few of the prisoners about coming up with a plan of attack, should a moment arise, but the more he looked around, the more discouraged he became.

These people were barely capable of functioning right now—not to mention they were less than friendly and he didn't want to take a chance on one of them giving him up. He hated to admit it, but there was nothing he could do right now but wait.

Allie's mother and the other prisoners had hardly finished their MREs when the three guards returned. The kid was assigned the task of unlocking the gate once more while the other two stood at the ready.

The woman took charge this time. "Let's go. Move it. Single file."

Tired groans came from the small crowd of prisoners as they began to shuffle toward the gate and line up.

"Just do what they say and they'll leave you alone," Sandy whispered.

"Probably best if they don't know you two are

mother and daughter," Ben replied quietly but unfortunately attracted the woman guard's attention.

"You two, up to the front so I can keep an eye on you." The woman was looking at him and Allie as she motioned with her gun for them to come forward.

Ben reluctantly headed to the front of the line. Allie walked behind him. He was proud of her for not making a scene while leaving her mother's side.

As they took their places at the front of the line, the man in civilian clothes ordered them to start walking. Ben and Allie led the way as they were escorted back through the tents and past the trailers along the same path they came in on.

As they approached the main gate, Ben noticed the last tent in the row had both of the large main flaps open, allowing him to see inside as they passed.

The tent was filled with personal items ranging from flat-screen TVs and furniture to gun safes and large garage toolboxes. Off to one side was an area of shelves filled with food, water, and a large collection of liquor bottles—all pilfered from the surrounding neighborhoods, no doubt.

The goods were all stacked up neatly in piles. These people either knew something he didn't or were complete idiots. Aside from the food and water, most of this stuff was worthless.

"Keep moving. Come on," the woman shouted.

Ben continued to lead the weary line out past the front gate. There, parked next to the Humvee, was one of the National Guards LMTVs (light medium tactical vehicle). The cargo truck had a canvas top that covered the rear trailer area. Ben could see through the rolled-up side panels that the truck was about half-full from the day's pillaging.

There were two more men with guns waiting by the back of the truck. They had a small step ladder leaning against the tailgate and motioned for Ben and Allie to climb into the truck.

One of the men leered at Allie as she climbed the ladder. "Hi there, sweetheart."

"Later." The other man pushed him and laughed as they both stepped aside a few feet to make room for the rest of the captives to form a line behind the truck.

There wouldn't be a later if Ben had anything to say about it. He eyeballed the two men as he climbed the ladder and stepped onto the truck bed.

A door slammed and a tall older man emerged from the trailer with the AC unit on top. He was the only one of the six that didn't have a rifle. Instead, he carried a large-caliber pistol on his side in a holster. He adjusted his tall black cowboy hat and sauntered down the steps from the trailer, letting his left hand rest on the holstered gun at his side as he walked.

"Let's see what we got today, shall we?" He boasted as he passed the original three guards that had brought the group out.

"Nice and easy now. Don't scratch nothin' up," one of the two men at the tailgate scolded.

Ben and Allie reluctantly began grabbing the items in the truck one by one and handing them down to the people on the ground, who in turn carried them to the tent for storage.

They started with the smaller things in the truck, and the whole time, Ben kept his eye out for anything he could use as a weapon. The man in the cowboy hat, who Ben presumed was their leader, had made his way into the watchtower to oversee the operation.

The three original guards were grouped together by the entrance to the camp and were busy smoking cigarettes and passing around a bottle of something. The two near the tailgate were the only ones half-heartedly paying attention to what was going on, and Ben noticed they were drinking as well.

They had moved most of the smaller things, and Ben helped Allie as they worked together now, lifting some of the larger pieces. He shook his head as he got one end of a large flat-screen TV. This was the most ridiculous thing he'd ever seen. He could feel his hatred for these people and what they were doing to them grow with each passing moment.

· 24 ·

Sandy was next in line so Ben and Allie handed down the large flat-screen to her and another guy. She managed a sad little grin at Allie as they handed off the TV.

Next up was a large garage toolbox. It was a nice unit with multiple drawers on top and a large cabinet on the bottom with casters. It looked heavy and he was glad to see it had wheels on it. He tugged on it and tried to roll it out from where it was wedged against the side of the truck, but it was very heavy and only moved a few inches on the uneven truck bed.

He put more effort into it this time and managed to make enough room for both him and Allie to get behind it. "Come around this side and help me push it, Allie."

She squeezed in next to him behind the massive tool chest and they began to push it toward the tailgate. Ben had no idea how they would get it down and out of the truck or how they had gotten the thing up there in the first place.

They picked up speed as they pushed until one of the wheels caught something on the floor. The cabinet came to an abrupt stop and began to tip. The upper cabinet must have been loaded with tools, since the whole thing was top-heavy and unbalanced.

He was able to catch it before it tipped too far and steadied it back on all four wheels. Taking a lower position on the cabinet, they started pushing toward the tailgate again. With all this work, Ben wasn't sure he'd have the energy to make an escape.

"Ahh!" The man in the cowboy hat yelped loudly from the watchtower and grabbed at his chest.

The dull crack of a distant rifle filled the air.

The man dropped out of sight behind the plywood half-wall and was gone.

Before any of the others had a chance to react, another shot rang out. This time, the man in civilian clothes near the front gate was the target. Ben saw a large chunk of the man's neck had been blown away.

The man grabbed at the wound in an effort to stop the heavy stream of blood shooting out, but it was no use. He looked at the other two with wide eyes as the blood oozed through his fingers.

"Help me," he gurgled, but he was done for by the time he hit the ground.

The young private was standing next to him when the bullet struck and had been caught in the bloody spray. He stood motionless, staring at the lifeless body on the ground.

It had to be Joel doing the shooting. But regardless of who it was, the time to capitalize on the moment was now.

"Push!" Ben yelled as he put everything he had behind the tool cabinet.

Allie joined him, and they gained speed quickly.

By the time the two men standing guard at the tailgate realized what was happening, it was too late. One of the men managed to get a couple shots off, but neither one penetrated the thick metal cabinet.

When Ben and Allie reached the end of the truck bed, the tool cabinet's wheels caught the edge like he'd hoped they would. The tool chest careened top-first over the edge and onto the men below with a sickening thud, crushing them both under its enormous weight.

The only two left standing now were the woman and kid pretending to be a private that had first intercepted Ben and Allie at the gate.

The kid began to shoot wildly in every direction as he tried to locate the source of the sniper, while the woman ran for cover back toward the camp.

She yelled for him to follow her, but he was oblivious to her calls and remained in the open. Locked in the moment and driven to panic by adrenaline and fear, the kid stood his ground, spraying bullets as fast as he could pull the trigger on the semiautomatic rifle.

Ben jumped down from the truck, pulling Allie with him. He glanced around but Sandy was nowhere to be seen.

"Stay down!" He grabbed a rifle from a bloody hand protruding out from under the tool cabinet. Instinctively, he thumbed the switch on the M4 to auto and dropped to the ground behind the truck near Allie. There was no time to think or feel sorry for the kid; he was going to kill somebody if he hadn't already.

Ben opened fire from his position under the truck. From where he was lying behind the rear wheels, he could only see him from the waist down. The first three-round burst tore into the kid's legs and quickly brought him to his knees.

Ben finished him off with another three-round burst to the upper torso before he had a chance to shoot back. His body jerked violently from the impact before he toppled over and fell limp on the pavement.

He quickly turned his attention to the woman, who was several yards into the camp by now. She was heading for the closest cover, which happened to be the tent they were using to store their loot.

He was about to take a shot when Allie's mother and the guy who had grumbled at them in the tent earlier appeared in the opening. They held the flat-screen TV over their heads, then heaved it down onto the woman as she was about to enter the tent. Preoccupied with the kid being gunned down, she never saw it coming—at least not until the last second, when she turned to go into the tent.

The large TV smashed her square in the face with so much force that it drove her backward and to the ground. Ben heard a loud crack upon impact and couldn't tell if it was the TV or her neck. She hit the ground hard with the TV landing on top of her, arms and legs still twitching in her final moments.

At least he knew Allie's mom was okay. He had lost track of her in the chaos and was concerned she'd been hit by the kid.

"Come on, Allie. Let's get your mom and get out of here." Ben helped her to her feet and they ran around the back of the truck toward Sandy.

"Are you okay?" Ben asked. Sandy stood there, staring at the woman on the ground without responding.

"Mom, are you okay?" Allie repeated.

"Yeah… Yes, I'm okay. I think." Sandy looked herself over.

"That was good thinking with the TV," Ben said. The man that had helped Sandy was back in the tent and loading a box with all the food and water he could carry.

With a crazed look on his face, he ran out of the tent and, without saying a word, took off down the road.

"That's not a bad idea. Let's grab what we can." Ben followed Allie and her mom into the tent and quickly found an empty box.

Sandy began to fill the box with MREs while Allie wrestled a case of water bottles down from the shelf. Ben grabbed a case of water himself and cradled it under his left arm. He wanted to keep his right hand free to use the gun just in case there was more trouble. There was a chance, after all, that it wasn't Joel doing the shooting.

"Only grab what you can carry by yourself," he warned as he peered out of the tent toward the road and the direction the shots had come from.

"Was that Joel?" Allie asked.

"I don't know. I think so, but until we're sure it's not someone else attacking the camp for supplies, we need to be careful." He thought about commandeering the Humvee and using it to get back to the Blazer. It sure would make carrying all this stuff a whole lot easier, especially for Sandy, who was already struggling with the box of food she had gathered.

Allie copied Ben's method for carrying the water and tucked the case she had under her arm so she could free up a hand for her mother.

"You can put it down for now. I want you to wait here while I search the trailer for keys to the Humvee. Maybe we can use it to get out of here." Ben peeked out from the tent again and surveyed the area. The trailer the leader had come out of most likely held the keys to all the vehicles. Most of the people had run into the nearby fields and were long gone. The rest were still hiding close by, unsure of what was going on.

Ben was about to run across the opening to the trailer when he heard a familiar sound. He looked down the road toward the interstate exit, and through the heat rising off the road, he saw the blurry image of a truck speeding toward them. It took him a moment to recognize the distorted image, but there was no mistaking it.

It was Joel in the Blazer.

"Change of plans, guys. Grab your stuff and follow me!"

Allie and her mom grabbed what they had just set down and moved over behind Ben at the door.

"It's Joel! He's coming to us." Ben took another quick look around outside the tent before stepping into the open lane that led out of camp.

"Now!" He motioned with his head for Allie and Sandy to follow him.

The women tried their best to stay close behind as they struggled with the supplies. Slowly but surely, they moved toward the front gate and the road beyond.

Ben kept an eye on the watchtower as they passed through the entrance. The guy in the cowboy hat had gone down pretty hard, but Ben wasn't about to let his guard down now. They were too close to make foolish mistakes.

He took a position behind Allie and her mom, putting himself between them and the camp. He meticulously checked every corner and crevice for trouble as they pushed on past the gate and the initial checkpoint. He backpedaled as he followed them out past the bodies.

For the first time, he noticed that a few of the prisoners had been shot and killed also—a result of the kid's panic-induced shooting spree. He tried to stay focused on the camp behind them. The end was in sight now.

All they had to do was get to the truck.

· 25 ·

Ben could see Joel in the driver's seat, with Gunner riding shotgun, as the truck sped toward them. Joel slammed on the brakes when he was about 40 yards out, causing the Blazer to break into a screeching sideways slide before coming to a complete stop. He flew out of the driver's seat, still wielding Ben's M24.

"Are you guys all right?" he yelled as he threw the rifle across the hood of the truck and got behind it.

Ben could hear the nervousness in his voice, but he never would have known it by his actions. "We're good. Is the truck open?"

"Yes," he answered.

Trusting that Joel had them covered, Ben slung the M4 over his shoulder and took the other case of water from Allie. He ran ahead to the truck and threw both cases in the back before running back to help them with the box of food.

"I got it. You guys get in the truck." Ben

grabbed the box from them and ran it the rest of the way to the truck, allowing the women to make better time.

Gunner was anxiously waiting on the front passenger seat to greet Allie when she opened the door. He quickly jumped to the back to make way for her and her mom to get in. Gunner barked nervously at Sandy a couple times before settling in on the bench seat next to Allie.

"It's okay, boy. We're here." Allie rubbed his head.

Ben finished cramming the box into the back and ran around to the driver's seat. "I'll drive, Joel. You cover us."

"Got it," Joel replied as he slipped around the front of the truck and got in on the other side.

Ben threw it into drive as soon as he sat down and handed the M4 to Joel. He pulled the door closed as they drove off and headed for the open highway.

A couple miles down the road and back on the interstate, they caught their breath and Allie began to make introductions.

"Mom, this is Joel. Joel, this is my mother, Sandy."

Joel twisted around in his seat and smiled. "Hi."

"Nice to meet you, Joel, and thank you for coming to get us, and thank you for taking care of my daughter."

Joel blushed as he nodded.

"Yes, thank you both for helping me get my mom back!" Allie grinned as Gunner nudged at her hand in an attempt to get scratched. "And this big guy here is Gunner. He's saved me from trouble more times than I'd like to admit."

Sandy's eyes widened.

Ben checked behind them again and confirmed that no one was coming before he backed off on the gas pedal. There were a few wrecked cars coming up and he needed to slow down. He looked over at Joel for the first time since he started driving and began nodding in approval.

"I'm proud of you. You did good back there, Son." He put his hand on Joel's shoulder.

"I didn't have much choice. I was watching through the scope and then I saw your signal. So I moved the truck closer and found a spot in the weeds near enough to take a shot if I got the chance. I would have waited there all night if I had to." Joel looked down at the floor, then back at Allie, who was talking to her mom. "I just imagined they were targets at the range!" he added before looking over at his dad.

"Well, you did the right thing. We wouldn't have made it out of there without you!" Ben did his best to reassure Joel of his actions. Doing a thing like that because it had to be done didn't make it easy. Taking a life never was, no matter how deserving the target might seem.

Ben noticed a transformation in his son, now more than ever. And although he could tell Joel was shaken from the rescue, he was somehow different than he had been in the past. Ben wasn't sure if numb was the right word, but there was a certain callousness to Joel's demeanor.

Ben remembered how the incident back in Colorado had affected him. He could tell Joel was deeply upset after being forced to shoot one of the guys who had abducted Allie. It had taken some time for Joel to accept what he'd done then. But now he seemed more than willing to put it behind him. That worried Ben because he knew that path, and it was a dangerous one.

"Hey, Allie, how about grabbing everyone a couple of waters from the back, if you can reach them?" Ben asked.

"Oh my gosh, I totally forgot. Joel, you must be so thirsty. And you too, Gunner." She twisted around in her seat and started handing bottles to everyone.

"Yes, thank you," Joel said.

Allie's movement interrupted Gunner from his position across her lap, and he shifted his weight onto Sandy. Allie filled his bowl with water and set it on the center console so he could reach it. He drank noisily until the bowl was empty. Allie filled it again and he finished most of that as well.

With water still dripping from his lips, Gunner

sat back on the seat and slumped over into Sandy's lap. He twisted around onto his back and exposed his belly to her.

Allie laughed. "I think he likes you."

Gunner's eyes closed as Sandy gave in and scratched him. "He reminds me of Molly a little bit." Sandy looked at Allie and began to tear up.

"Molly was our dog in Pittsburgh. She stayed there with Allie's dad when we moved," she explained to Joel and Ben.

"Oh yeah. Allie told me she had a yellow Lab at her dad's," Joel answered.

"Sweetie, I need to tell you something about your dad." Sandy cleared her throat before continuing. "I talked to some of the people at the FEMA camp when we first got there, before it was taken over. The people with the National Guard told me that Pittsburgh was gone. Your dad... I think your dad is..." She broke down in tears and couldn't get the words out.

Allie leaned over, embracing her mother as they both cried.

"I know. We heard about Pittsburgh." Allie sniffled.

"Your dad loved you very much. I want you to know that. And I'm sorry for taking you away from him," Sandy apologized.

"I know he did. It's not your fault, Mom. It's okay." Allie shook her head.

Allie and her mom continued to talk quietly in the back seat as they drove on. Ben heard bits and pieces of the conversation as Allie filled her in on the highlights of their journey.

Joel seemed content to stare out the window and enjoy the breeze. After what had just happened, Ben figured it was best to leave him to his thoughts for now.

He was enjoying the relative quiet of the truck, and even though the air coming in his window was still hot, he was satisfied to be moving east again.

The interstate was mostly open except for the occasional blockage, but the wide shoulders and center median made it easy to get around them when necessary. It was almost four in the afternoon, but he knew if they could push on for just another hour or so, they could make it to West Virginia.

There was no reason to stop until they were done for the day, now that they had water. They would just have to make sure they spent the night somewhere with a water source. But what they had would be more than enough to get them through the night if necessary.

· 26 ·

Ben was encouraged by the changing landscape as the flat open fields gave way to the foothills of the Appalachian Mountains. The long straight sections of highway were becoming less and less frequent with each passing mile now that they were getting back into the mountains.

It made driving a little more challenging, and he knew the Blazer would go through fuel at a faster rate with the constant elevation changes. But in spite of the new challenges, he still felt a small sense of relief to be back in familiar terrain.

"Wow, West Virginia already?" Joel read the sign as they passed.

"Yeah, it's only another hour to Pennsylvania from here. But I think we can start looking for a place to camp anytime now. I was hoping to make it there today, but all things considered, I think we did pretty well."

"I agree." Joel nodded.

"Besides, I'm sure you guys are ready to stretch your legs." Ben glanced in the rearview mirror at Allie and her mom. The back seat wasn't really set up for two people and a large dog right now, but they could fix that.

Sandy spoke up. "Yeah, that would be nice, but we can manage as long as you want to keep going."

"We'll do a little rearranging before we get back on the road tomorrow and try to get you guys a little more room back there. I think I can get almost everything in the back. It'll be tight, but we can make it work," Ben promised.

"We may have to strap a few more things to the roof," Joel added.

"We may have to," Ben agreed. He knew it was a temporary solution. They were slowly outgrowing the Blazer and it would only get worse once they got to Maryland. The thought of finding some type of camper they could tow came to mind again—something lightweight that the Blazer could pull without too much trouble.

Traveling through the mountains with a camper wouldn't be ideal, but they were running out of options. They would make do without it for as long as they could. Towing a camper would also mean stopping for gas more often and being a lot less maneuverable on the highway.

Ben thought back to all the times in the past week or so that they had been forced to evade trouble on the road. The outcome for all of those instances would have been much different had they been towing a camper. The more he thought about it, the less he liked the idea.

The idea of finding a bigger truck or a second truck might be the way to go. Of course, finding something that was in good running condition was another challenge altogether.

He had briefly considered taking the Humvee from the FEMA camp but ultimately decided that it would be a mistake. The biggest reason was that if they ran into legitimate National Guard troops, it wouldn't look too good, and they would, at the very least, take it back.

The other reason was the scarcity of parts for the diesel-powered Humvee—not to mention that Ben wasn't familiar with the mechanics of a Humvee and didn't think he could make repairs as easily as he could to the Blazer or an older-model truck.

Joel, who was leaning forward and looking out the front window at something, interrupted Ben's thoughts.

"What about down there?" Joel pointed.

Up ahead was a small bridge that crossed over a stream. There was a dirt road off to the side of the interstate that led down alongside the bridge to the water's edge. The stream itself sat down below the interstate in a gully that ran parallel to the highway above.

Ben slowed down and kept close to the edge of the bridge as they crossed over the water. They could see a good distance in both directions as they checked up and down the stream. Ben looked at the water closely as they passed over.

"Water seems good," he said.

"It's actually sorta clear. I can see the bottom," Joel remarked.

It was the nicest water they'd seen since Colorado, and it reminded Ben of the rivers and streams back home, only smaller.

By the time they had reached the end of the bridge, he was convinced to give the place a try. The clean water was reason enough to stay here, but the possibilities of fresh trout for dinner played a big factor as well.

He steered the Blazer through the tall grassy shoulder of the interstate and forged a path down to the dirt road alongside the bridge.

Gunner had been awake and sitting up between Allie and her mom on the back seat since they'd slowed down to look at the stream. He was beside himself with excitement and panted heavily between whines of anticipation. Gunner would have to wait a little longer, though.

Unlike the bridge they'd slept under before, this one wasn't large enough to conceal the truck from potential traffic on the interstate above.

"We better look for a spot away from the

highway." Ben steered the truck left and followed the overgrown dirt trail downstream.

They bounced along for half a mile or so until he saw a clearing suitable to set up camp. It was close to the water and he'd be able to keep an eye on everybody and everything from one spot.

"This looks good," Allie said.

Ben parked the truck and got out. Gunner seized the opportunity and leapt over the center console and out the driver's side door. Ben watched the dog as he zipped around the edge of the clearing.

"I'd say the leg is all healed." Joel laughed as he got out of the truck and stretched.

Allie and her mom climbed out behind him.

Gunner hit the water with a splash as he launched himself off a rock and into a deep pool of water. He swam a few circles before heading back to shore and shaking off, the bandage barely clinging to his leg.

"Come here, boy." Allie called the dog over. Gunner came trotting over with a pleased look on his face and allowed her to inspect his leg. She smiled. "I don't think we need to replace the bandage. It looks pretty good to me. Just two small scabs, but the swelling is gone. I guess whatever Reese gave him really helped."

Ben climbed up to the rooftop cargo box and started to unload. He was glad now that he had brought a few extra sets of gear.

"Sandy, you can use these. Here's a sleeping pad, a bag, and a one-person bivy. Allie can show you how to set it up." Ben handed the items down to her, along with Allie's gear.

Ben grabbed the rest of his and Joel's stuff and was about to close the box when Joel stopped him.

"Want me to try to catch a few fish for dinner?" Joel asked.

"Yeah, I guess so. That'd be great." Ben handed Joel his rod and bag before closing the lid and jumping down.

"I'll head upstream. I can't really fish here." Joel looked at the brown stain in the water as it followed the current downstream in front of the campsite. The water was still heavy with silt from Gunner's cannonball attempt just a minute ago.

"Don't go far, okay?" Ben asked. It had been a big day, and as much as Joel probably needed this, Ben still wanted to play it conservative for the night. He didn't want him going far or being out of his sight for very long.

"Got it." Joel started upstream, picking his way over the rocks.

Gunner followed, calmer now that he had gotten the initial burst of energy out of his system. He was more than happy to bring up the rear and explore the crevices between the larger boulders with his nose. Within a minute, both Joel and the dog were out of sight.

Ben started with Joel's tent first while Allie helped her mom get set up.

"Fire or stove tonight?" Allie asked.

Ben thought for a minute. The area looked pretty isolated from people and it would be nice to save the gas.

"I'll build a small fire. I think we'll be all right here," he announced. It would keep any four-legged intruders away as well, although he didn't want to mention that part to the girls at the moment.

Anything he could do to help ensure an uneventful night seemed like a good idea right now.

As soon as he finished setting up his tent and squaring away his gear, he started digging the two small holes for the fire. It probably wasn't the fire Allie was hoping for, but it was a compromise he could feel good about. He wanted to eliminate as much smoke as possible and reduce the visibility of the fire.

While he worked on the fire, Allie showed her mother the pots and pans and went over how they typically prepared their meals.

Without skipping a beat, she gathered the water filter and empty Nalgene bottles from the truck and took her mom down to the water and demonstrated how the filtration system worked. When they came back from the stream, they had all the bottles filled with fresh cold water. Allie handed him one of the still-dripping bottles as they walked by him on the way back to the truck.

Ben could hear Allie explaining the Dakota two-hole method he was using to make their fire for the night. Ben smiled. He was proud of Allie and recognized the change in her since reuniting with her mother at the camp.

Finding her mom was extremely lucky, and he was thankful for it. It meant another mouth to feed, but that was a small price to pay to see Allie return to her old self. He had to admit it was nice to have another adult around, too.

He had been worried about Allie and the news of Pittsburgh looming over her like a dark cloud. It was the boost she needed, and he wasn't sure if she would have made it otherwise. But now, he saw new life in her eyes. The sad blank stare had been replaced with hope.

He still wasn't looking forward to passing through the section of I-70 that would take them by Pittsburgh. It was less than 30 miles from the city at the closest point, and if the place had been hit as bad as what they'd heard, it wouldn't be pretty. It would be confirmation that her dad hadn't made it.

Having her mother by her side would help soften the blow—at least that was what he hoped.

· 27 ·

They were losing the last light of the day as Gunner tore into camp and headed straight for Allie. Ben was relieved to see that Joel wasn't far behind and had three decent-sized trout strung through their gills on a small branch.

"All cleaned and ready to go," he announced proudly.

Sandy smiled. "Wow, you guys really have your act together."

"Joel could pull a fish out of a mud puddle," Ben joked. "He's always been lucky that way. Even as a little kid, he always managed to find fish. It never ceased to amaze me."

Joel shook his head, clearly embarrassed by what his dad had said. He handed the fish off to Allie before stowing away his rod and bag.

She wrapped the trout in foil and laid them over the fire on the grate next to the pot of water.

Joel came back from the truck with a bowl of dog food and set it down nearby.

Gunner shot up from where he was lying, immediately abandoning the stick he had been chewing on. He trotted over and made quick work of the bowl of food. Looking back at Joel as he chewed the last mouthful, he realized that was all he was getting for now. He found a spot by the fire and made a few circles before finally settling down on the ground with a grunt.

"Maybe there'll be some leftovers, boy." Joel shrugged as he joined the rest of them around the fire. They sat in silence for a couple minutes, watching the flames dance up through the metal cooking grate while they waited for the water to boil and the fish to cook. Ben could feel the fire lulling him into a trance as the day began to catch up to him. He'd have no trouble sleeping tonight.

Sandy broke the silence. "This is really nice compared to the way I've been living lately."

"It doesn't always go this smooth," Joel quipped.

"Yeah, I heard. Allie filled me in on your adventures so far. It's hard to believe that people have resorted to doing the things they're doing. I never would have thought that society and basic human decency would deteriorate so quickly."

"Adventures is a much nicer word than I would use." Ben sighed. "We've had our share of close calls, but I'll say this: without these two, we wouldn't be sitting here right now. I couldn't have asked for two better partners," he bragged.

Allie smiled as she got up and added two packets of dehydrated food to the pot of boiling water, along with some seasoning and fresh vegetables. "I think that has more to do with you than us." She looked at Ben as she continued to stir the pot.

"Don't be so quick to sell yourself short," Ben objected. "You guys have been a big help to me."

"Don't forget Gunner!" Allie smiled.

At the sound of his name, Gunner lifted his head from where he lay next to the fire and looked in her direction. He stared at her sleepily for a moment and wagged his tail a few times before putting his head back down.

Joel checked on the fish and saw that it was ready. He slowly and carefully removed the bones and flaked the meat off into the pot, mixing it in with the beans and rice.

"I hope that was okay. I mean, do you like trout?" Joel raised an eyebrow at Sandy.

"Oh, it's fine. It smells great. You'll get no complaints from me after what I've been eating," Sandy answered.

She shook her head as she continued. "I really can't thank you enough, Ben. Or you, Joel. You've done so much for me and my daughter. Whatever I can do to help you get to your kids in Maryland, just let me know." She leaned over, put her arm around Allie, and pulled her close. "You've given me a reason to live again," she finished with a tearful eye.

Ben and Joel both smiled back at her and nodded. It made Ben feel good to see Allie and her mom together. It gave him hope that anything was possible. Reuniting with Bradley and Emma seemed somehow closer to becoming a reality and more achievable now than ever.

If they could maintain this pace and manage to avoid any more trouble, they could get really close tomorrow. He kept running over the map in his mind as Joel and Allie divided up the food onto plates and handed it out.

He still hadn't decided on a route to the eastern shore of Maryland. The more direct and dangerous way could potentially get them there as soon as tomorrow night with a little luck. They would have to drive later than they usually did, but it was doable.

But that meant crossing the Chesapeake Bay Bridge.

"Oh my gosh! This is really good. I mean, it's so much better than I expected. Wait, that sounded bad." Sandy smiled. "It's just that this is the first real food I've had in a while."

They all laughed a little, and for the first time in a while, things didn't seem so bad. The feeling was short-lived, though, and Ben found himself engrossed in thoughts of tomorrow yet again.

He remembered the Chesapeake Bay Bridge being two separate bridges, actually: three lanes west and two lanes east. It was also a very long and very tall bridge. And he couldn't help but wonder about the structural integrity of it.

If D.C. had been hit hard, would the shockwaves damage the bridge? It was less than 50 miles from D.C., as the crow flew. And damage wasn't the least of his concerns.

There was a good chance that it was blocked as well. They might not even be able to get across. It was the only way over the Chesapeake Bay without going north or south a good distance, so it was a busy bridge that saw heavy truck traffic from the surrounding cities.

The alternative was to go north and make their way around the bay, bringing them down through Delaware. That route had the benefit of avoiding Baltimore and D.C. altogether rather than running directly between the two.

But it would add time—time Ben was reluctant to give up. In his gut, he knew going around was the way to go. The bridge was too risky, and if they couldn't cross it, they'd have to drive around to the north anyway.

"That sure hit the spot," Joel exclaimed as he got up with his empty plate.

They had all finished their meals entirely, except for Allie, who had a couple spoonfuls left. She scrapped it off her plate and into Gunner's bowl, where he was already waiting anxiously in anticipation of the leftovers.

"There you go, boy." Allie rubbed his head as she got up, leaving him to enjoy his treat.

"I'll do the dishes. I wanted to clean up a little anyway," Sandy offered.

"I'll help you. I want to wash up, too." Allie gathered the utensils and plates while Sandy grabbed the pot and Gunner's already-empty bowl. The two headed off to the stream, Gunner close behind.

"I'll grab some more wood for the fire if we're going to keep it going," Joel offered.

Ben nodded. "Yeah, I'll give you a hand. I'd like to let it burn for as long as we can. No need to stay up to keep it going or anything like that. Just enough to keep the critters away for a while." He was too tired to think about it anymore tonight. Joel could drive first thing tomorrow and he could spend some time looking over the map.

He and Joel found a few nice pieces of wood that he thought could be stuffed into the fire pit but were big enough to last a few hours. Ben went about setting up the fire for a long slow burn while Joel dug a hole and buried their trash from dinner.

"Joel, you want to drive for a while tomorrow? It'll give me a chance to look at the map a little more. I think we need to find an alternative to going over the Chesapeake Bay Bridge."

"Sure, no problem," Joel answered as Allie and her mom returned from the stream.

Sandy yawned. "Oh, I feel much better now. All I need is some sleep and I might start to feel human again."

"I was going to try to reorganize the truck tonight, but I think it'll have to wait until morning. I just don't have it in me. Let's stow everything and lock up for the night." Ben stifled a yawn of his own. "Besides, we've got a big day ahead tomorrow and I want to get started early."

"Getting some rest sounds like a good idea," Sandy agreed as she and Allie loaded what they had into the back of the Blazer.

Ben closed the tailgate behind them and locked the doors before heading for his tent. He checked the fire one more time while he brushed his teeth. Satisfied with how it was burning, he finished up and rinsed his mouth out with fresh cold stream water before he climbed halfway into his tent and took his boots off.

Gunner had already decided who he was sleeping with and was sitting outside Allie's tent, waiting patiently for an opportunity to get inside. As soon as she unzipped the flap, he disappeared inside for the evening. They all said good night to one another and retreated to their tents.

Ben laid back and tried to quiet his mind over the concerns of tomorrow. They still had a distance to go yet, but they were close now, and that gave him some satisfaction. It wasn't long before the gurgling stream and chirping frogs lured him into a deep sleep.

· 28 ·

Allie awoke to the sound of gear being moved around in the truck. Gunner was already up and whining faintly as he looked at her to let him out of the tent. She unzipped the flap and he squeezed out through the narrow opening as soon as it was big enough to get his head through.

As she opened it the rest of the way, she saw Ben had the back of the Blazer open and was sorting through gear. There were a few piles on the ground and the rooftop cargo box was open as well.

The pleasant aroma of fresh-brewed coffee was a welcome smell and made the prospect of getting up and out of the tent a little less painful. She lingered for a minute longer at the door of her tent, stretching and taking in the morning, not quite ready to get her shoes on and admit to herself that it was time to get moving.

The sun was barely up and the woods were just

starting to come alive with the sound of birds singing in the distance.

Gunner came back around from wherever he had run off to and shoved a cold nose at her face. He leaned into her, half-wet from his morning foray through the tall dew-covered grass.

"Oh, Gunner! Good morning to you, too," Allie complained with a smile.

She reluctantly pulled her shoes on and got to her feet. Ben's tent was already packed up and she noticed the flap on Joel's tent was pulled back. It was empty and had a rolled-up sleeping bag sitting inside. Her mom's tent was the only one still zipped up, and Allie assumed she was still sleeping.

Allie headed over to the Blazer, where she could see the back half of Ben sticking out of the truck while he rearranged the gear. "Good morning."

"Morning. How'd you sleep?" he asked.

"I must have slept pretty well. I don't remember a thing." She smiled.

"Me too. Joel's down by the water, getting cleaned up. Your mom is still sleeping, but I think we should let her go for a while. She's had a rough couple of days." Ben handed a mug to Allie from the back of the truck.

"Okay. Oh, thanks. I could use some coffee." Allie took the cup and headed over to the fire.

"There should be enough left. I've had a few cups already this morning." Ben grinned.

"No problem. I'll make more and get started on breakfast while I'm at it."

Allie fought the urge to wake her mother up. It wasn't that she didn't want her to sleep, but she wanted to make sure she hadn't dreamt yesterday. She still couldn't believe that she had her mother back. She wasn't alone anymore.

Of course, she knew she was never alone with Joel and Ben, but this was different. This was family. Ever since she found out about Pittsburgh, her emotions had been on a roller-coaster.

And she would be kidding herself if she didn't admit that there was a point where she wasn't sure if she was going to make it. She hadn't felt sure if any of them were going to make it. But now there was reason to have hope for the future.

Maybe everything was going to work out. Maybe they would find Joel's brother and sister and all get back to Colorado. As she drank her coffee, the warmth seemed to spill over into her mood. She felt like anything was possible today.

"Good morning!" Joel chirped.

"Oh, good morning!" She was so engrossed in her thoughts that she hadn't noticed him approaching.

"Sorry. Didn't mean to startle you."

"It's fine. I'm not really awake yet." She gave him a sleepy wink.

"I'll give you a hand with breakfast."

"Thanks. I was just getting ready to make some more coffee. I know my mom will want some," she replied.

Gunner ran over to greet Joel and give him a good sniffing over.

"No swimming for you this morning! Nobody wants to smell wet dog all day in the truck." Joel looked at Gunner as he rubbed his head.

"Yeah, especially now that things are a little tight in there," Allie added.

"Hopefully my dad can move things around and make some room." Joel walked over to the truck and inspected his dad's work.

Allie joined him and started gathering what they would need for breakfast.

Ben had gotten nearly everything tucked into the rear of the truck. There was still a large duffel bag sitting on the ground filled with MREs and dehydrated food pouches.

"Where's that going?" Joel asked.

"On the roof. It's all sealed in plastic bags anyway." He shrugged. "It opened up a lot of space and makes things easier to get to."

Allie pulled out two large pouches marked as brown sugar and maple oatmeal from the duffel bag and threw them into the pot she was already holding.

"Wow, that does make a big difference!" She looked inside the truck.

"I'm trying to make a spot for Gunner in the back on the gear. That way you and your mom can have the back seat to yourselves."

"Thanks. That's great! Although I don't think Gunner's going to be too happy about that!" She raised an eyebrow.

Gunner heard his name and instantly appeared at the back of the truck, watching Ben. He let out a sharp bark, followed by a whine.

"Looks like somebody else is ready for breakfast, too!" Joel grabbed Gunner's bowl from a nearby bush, where it hung from last night's cleaning. He scooped a couple handfuls of dry food into it and put it on the ground.

Gunner gave it a few sniffs and dug in.

Allie heard a zipper, followed by her mother's voice.

"Morning!" Sandy rubbed her eyes as she emerged from the tent. Gunner stopped eating and trotted over to Sandy, wagging his tail. He greeted her briefly with a couple soft growls and then quickly headed back to his bowl to finish eating.

"Is that coffee I smell?" she asked.

"Yes, it is. I'm getting ready to make more now, along with breakfast." Allie handed her mother the still-steaming, half-full mug she was drinking. "Here. You can have this."

"Thanks. You should have gotten me up sooner. I want to help out." Sandy frowned.

"You can help Allie with breakfast if you want. I'll go fill the waters while you guys do that," Joel offered.

"Okay, great." Sandy smiled and joined Allie by the fire.

Gunner finished eating and followed Joel down to the water. Allie and her mom got breakfast started while Ben put the finishing touches on the truck and secured the duffel bag to the rack.

Allie should have been content. It was a good morning—at least as good as they got these days. But something was bothering her. She was dreading the fact that they were going to pass by Pittsburgh today. The news they had heard about Pittsburgh was true; she could feel it in her gut. It had to be. They'd heard it from too many different sources.

She knew her dad was gone, but passing by the city today would make it real.

· 29 ·

Ben filled them in on his plans for the day over breakfast and explained why he thought the Chesapeake Bay Bridge should be avoided. They all agreed with his idea of taking a northern route around the bay and down through Delaware.

They quickly cleaned up after breakfast and loaded the remaining gear.

"Joel, you still feel like driving this morning?" Ben asked.

"Yep! No problem." He caught the keys as Ben tossed them in his direction. Joel climbed into the driver's seat while Gunner hopped up into the truck and made his way to the back seat.

Allie and her mom followed.

"Come on, boy. Here you go." Allie patted her hand on the pile of blankets Ben had made over the gear in the back. Gunner reluctantly climbed over the seat as Allie continued to coax him onto the makeshift dog bed. He settled in with a grunt and stretched his neck out so that he could still rest his head on the back of their seat.

"Oh my, what a sad look!" Sandy smiled as she rubbed Gunner behind the ears. As Ben got situated in the passenger seat, he looked at the pathetic display Gunner was putting on for the girls and shook his head.

"He'll be fine. He's got the best spot in the truck," Ben joked.

Joel followed the overgrown trail back out to the interstate and headed east. It wasn't long until they saw a sign for Pennsylvania. At only 58 miles away, Pittsburgh was among the destinations listed on the sign.

Ben wondered how long before they would start to see signs of the devastation they had heard about. If they were lucky, they would only skirt the edge of it. They would be closest as they made their way around the town of Washington, Pennsylvania. The interstate ran around the town to the north and looked to be only about 15 miles from Pittsburgh, according to the map.

If the city had in fact been ground zero for a nuclear detonation, they would know for sure.

"How far do you think we'll get today?" Joel asked.

"It depends how long we drive. I think we're going to be close enough that if we push on a little later than normal, we'll be able to make it there late tonight. Of course, that's assuming the roads are decent." Ben looked at the map as he spoke.

"Really? I thought we were still a day or two away?" Joel sounded surprised.

Ben shook his head. "Not if we get a good day of driving in."

Sandy cleared her throat. "I've been wanting to say something since last night but never got the chance. I don't want to keep you from your kids any longer. You've already done enough to keep my daughter safe and to help her find me. If Pittsburgh is truly gone, then there's no point in wasting time there. I want you to just drive on by when we get there. I insist."

Ben turned in his seat to look at Sandy and was going to tell her that they would wait and see what they found before making any decisions, but before he could say anything, Allie chimed in.

"My mom's right. We need to get to Bradley and Emma, and you know it. Even if Pittsburgh is okay, we need to keep going. We're coming back this way, right?" She nodded at Ben. "We can stop on the way back to Colorado."

"We'll see." That was all Ben could think to say. He turned back around in his seat and looked out the window. They were right, and he knew it. It was time to get to the kids.

The trip had already taken longer than he expected. It had been nine days of hard traveling, and if he was being honest, the last thing he wanted to do was delay things anymore by getting sidetracked in Pittsburgh. He felt bad for Allie, but maybe it was for the best to keep moving and put Pittsburgh behind them.

Especially if that was what she and her mom wanted.

Joel continued east through the rolling hills of western Pennsylvania. The rhythmic sound of the tires humming on the pavement and the drone of the engine were the only sounds inside the truck.

Sandy looked a little better today, but it was going to take her a while to recover from her weakened condition. Ben could tell she was still suffering from a lack of proper nutrition. She had fallen asleep already and was leaning against the cab of the truck. He was sure she wouldn't have lasted much longer at the camp if they hadn't found her when they did.

"Look, another truck!" Joel pointed to the westbound lane as an old Toyota pickup with a loaded bed went flying by in the other direction.

"Looks like they've got some mechanical problems," Ben commented. There was a faint trail of smoke behind the vehicle.

"Probably burning oil. They won't last long running like that," Joel added.

Ben looked closer and realized it wasn't smoke at all. It was dust. Why would they be leaving a trail of dust on the paved interstate?

He checked the side mirror on his door and saw that they were also kicking up a thick trail of dust behind the Blazer, as well as leaving tire tracks on the road. It reminded him of how it looked when driving through a light layer of freshly fallen snow on the road.

But this wasn't snow.

"What is that on the road?" Allie asked.

"It's like a powder or something," Joel said.

Ben leaned out the window and watched the road pass by underneath. The front tires pushed out the fine, grayish-brown material as they went. It had the consistency of a thick fine powder and almost seemed to be in a liquid state as it was forced away from the tire.

Then it hit him what they were driving through.

"It's nuclear fallout. Allie, give me an old towel from the back and let's get the windows up."

Allie handed Ben a towel, which he proceeded to cut up into pieces with his knife while Joel rolled up his window.

Ben handed the pieces to Allie. "Get these damp so we can use them to breathe through until we get out of this." Allie poured a small amount of water over the pile of towel pieces and handed them out to everyone.

"Mom, wake up!" Allie shook her mom's shoulder gently.

"What's going on?" Sandy mumbled.

"You need to breathe through this." Allie handed her the piece of damp towel as she covered her mouth and nose with her own piece.

"What about Gunner?" Allie asked.

"Try to keep him covered as best you can," Ben said.

Allie took a piece of the towel and slowly draped it over Gunner's snoot while rubbing his head.

"Easy, boy. It's okay," she said.

He resisted at first and pawed at the towel over his nose, but Allie was persistent. He finally gave in and accepted the makeshift mask.

Ben could see it now in the trees and on the waist-high grass along the side of the road. It was getting thicker by the mile, and soon everything was covered in the fine ash. The trees and plants were all dead or dying, and Ben knew without a doubt this was the result of a nuclear detonation.

As they followed the interstate around Washington, Pennsylvania, the effects of the blast became more and more evident. The wrecks they passed by had been blown off the road and were lying in the median or on the shoulder. Most were lying on their sides or on their roofs.

Ben wasn't sure if it was his imagination or if it was real, but the trees looked like they were all leaning to the west a few degrees. Could the shockwave from the blast have caused that this far away? And if it had, then there was definitely nothing left of Pittsburgh. They needed to get through here as fast as they could. He instantly regretted being this close as it was.

"Is this radioactive?" Sandy asked.

"I don't know. It's possible." Ben had thought about that, but there was no way of being sure. There were too many unknown factors.

"It depends on the design of the weapon, the detonation altitude, and the weather conditions. Pittsburgh itself will still be radioactive for sure, and there'll be hot spots around this area that will pose a high radiation hazard. The best thing to do is get far away from this area as quickly as possible," Ben stated.

His knowledge of nuclear weapons was limited, but he knew enough about residual radiation to know it was best to steer clear of this place. It could be a radioactive hot spot for years to come. Even the soil could be contaminated, and he wouldn't be surprised if everything in the immediate area eventually died off. He hoped they hadn't been exposed to any radiation.

Nobody said a word as they passed by the Pittsburgh exit. There was no need for any further discussion about the matter.

Allie's father was gone and so was the city.

· 30 ·

Within a matter of 10 or 15 minutes after passing the Pittsburgh exit, the fallout began to thin. The trees slowly returned to their normal color and the layer of ash on the road grew thinner until it was gone.

The trees and grass had a dry, parched look as the greens of summer were replaced with wilted brown in many areas, but it was a welcome sight compared to the gray, ash-covered trees. He was glad to be past the worst of it and made a quick note on the map.

Another place to avoid on the way back to Colorado, he thought.

He wasn't surprised that the trees and plants looked like this. They hadn't seen much rain since they'd started their journey. It had been nine days of hot, dry weather.

The water levels of the rivers and streams they passed over and camped at hadn't gone unnoticed by him. Last night, he saw the old water line on the rocks along the bank. In fact, everywhere they had been in the last couple days looked to be well below the normal water level. Had the bombs somehow affected the weather? Was that even possible?

He was mad at himself for letting them get this close. They should've gone farther south and heeded the warnings they were given. Most of the health problems brought on by radiation were from long-term exposure. If they were exposed, hopefully the dose was minimal and they passed through quickly enough to avoid any serious effects.

"Can we take these down now?" Allie asked.

Ben pulled the towel from his face "Yeah, it should be okay now. I just didn't want anyone to breathe in those particles. That's bad stuff!"

Gunner let out a loud sneeze when Allie removed the towel from his snoot. Glad to be free of the restriction, he belly-crawled toward Allie and her mom until he could hang his front paws over the back of the seat along with his head.

"Can we open the windows again?" Joel asked.

"Yes, please." Ben rolled his window down and Joel did the same. Although the air was warm, it cooled the truck a little as it rushed in.

"Whew, that's better!" Sandy sighed as she used her piece of towel to wipe the sweat from her face.

"Sorry. We could have used the AC, but I didn't want to suck any of that in here with us," Ben said.

"It's fine. We're low on gas anyway," Joel added.

"How low?" Ben leaned over to peek at the fuel gauge.

"A little over a quarter tank," Joel answered.

"Well, I guess we better start looking." They had all been too preoccupied with the devastation outside to notice they were running low on gas—not that they would have stopped anywhere back there if they had noticed. Ben didn't like being this low on fuel, especially when they were in the middle of nowhere like they were at the moment.

"How about we pull over if you can find some shade and we'll add the two spare cans to the tank." Ben looked at Joel.

"How about up there?" He pointed to an overpass that crossed the interstate up ahead.

"Sure," Ben answered. He surveyed the area as Joel slowed the truck and pulled in under the bridge. He felt the change in temperature immediately as the Blazer came to a stop in the shade.

Gunner was up immediately and whined impatiently at the opportunity to get out. As soon as Ben opened his door, Gunner launched himself over the rear seat between Allie and her mom. He cleared the center console and Ben's seat in a single bound. Within a few seconds, he had disappeared into the tall weeds along the road.

"Gunner! Don't go too far, boy," Joel called after the dog as he shut the truck off and climbed out.

"I'll leave the keys in the ignition so you can listen to the radio," he joked.

"Right, thanks." Allie laughed.

Ben already had the first spare fuel can unstrapped by the time Joel made his way to the back of the truck.

"Here you go." Ben handed him the spare and started to loosen the other one. Joel lugged the heavy tank around to the side of the truck and began to transfer the gas. Ben joined him with the other tank shortly.

"It feels kind of nice under here," Joel remarked.

"Yeah, it's not bad." Ben sighed as he leaned against the truck and took his sunglasses off. He pulled the piece of towel from his back pocket and wiped his face clean of sweat. There was a slight breeze, and it felt good in the shade of the overpass. It was the first real relief from the heat they'd had all day.

"Hey, guys. Listen!" Allie blurted out.

Joel stopped pouring gas and set the container down on the ground.

"What is it?" Ben asked. He didn't hear anything.

"The radio!" Allie answered. "There was a voice. I swear I heard a voice."

"I heard it, too," Sandy added.

Ben and Joel were now both standing at the open driver's door, staring at the illuminated radio.

"I turned it on and hit scan. I was just fooling around. I didn't think it would actually work." Allie's eyes were wide with disbelief.

"What did you hear?" Joel asked.

"There was a voice but then static and—" Allie was cut off by the sound of static and three short garbled electronic noises. Ben immediately recognized the sound as the EAS (Emergency Alert System) alarm. A computerized voice followed the signal with an announcement.

"We interrupt this program. This is a national emergency. Important instructions will follow."

There was a pause followed by a long higher-pitched tone before the monotone voice continued.

"The following message is being transmitted at the request of the United States government. This is not a test. A nuclear attack was commenced against the United States. Twenty-three nuclear bombs have been detonated in areas around the coun—"

The radio cut out as quickly as it had come on, leaving them all staring at it blankly. The frequencies started scrolling by as the radio resumed its search for a broadcasting channel.

They all looked at each other. Ben wasn't sure what to make of it other than that they now knew how many bombs had hit—if what they heard on the radio was even accurate.

"Check your phones." Ben looked at Joel, then Allie.

"Do you think they'll work? I haven't even been able to turn mine on since the morning it happened," Allie said.

"Joel and I had our phones turned off. We always keep them off when we're camping to save the battery in case we need it," Ben said.

Joel was already around the other side of the truck and digging through the glove box for his phone. He pulled it out and held the power button down. Within a few seconds, the screen lit up with a picture of Joel posing with a large brown trout.

"Brian took that." Joel swallowed as he waited for the phone to connect.

"Any signal?" Ben asked impatiently.

"Nothing." Joel shook his head. He stared at the screen for a moment before turning the phone off.

"What does it mean?" Sandy asked.

"I don't know, but it's something. It at least means they're trying to get communications back up and running." Ben headed back around to continue refueling. Joel tossed his phone back in the glove compartment and joined his dad.

Ben could hear the girls talking quietly among themselves while he and Joel finished pouring the last of the second can into the truck.

In the meantime, Gunner had come back from

his short-lived adventure in the grass and hopped into the truck on his own.

"Do you think things will ever be the way they were before?" Joel carried one of the empty gas tanks to the back of the truck and secured it in place.

Ben thought for a second before he answered. He didn't want to sound to negative, but he didn't want to lie, either.

"No, I don't think it will ever be the same, Joel, but I do think it'll get better."

· 31 ·

It wasn't what Joel wanted to hear, but he knew it was probably true. It never would be the same again. But like his dad said, things would get better. Exactly how long it would be before that happened was anyone's guess. One thing was for certain, though: some of these scars would never heal, and he'd never forget some of the things he'd had to do.

"I got this. Are you still good to drive?" Ben startled Joel at the back of the truck with the other empty can. He hadn't even noticed his dad coming.

"Yeah, I'm good for a while, I think. Maybe you can take over when we stop for gas."

"Sounds good." Ben nodded.

Joel left for the driver's seat while his dad strapped down the empty gas can. When he got back in the truck, Allie and her mom were talking quietly about something. Gunner was in the back, sprawled out in his new spot and panting heavily next to a freshly drained water bowl Allie must have given him.

He fired the truck up and checked the fuel gauge. They had a little over a half a tank now, and depending on the terrain, it should get them a couple hours of driving. Plenty of time to find a place to top off all the tanks.

Ben hopped into the passenger's seat and closed the door. "We ought to make Maryland within the hour."

"How much gas do we have?" Allie asked.

"Just over half a tank. Maybe a couple hours' worth of driving," Joel answered.

"We'll hit mountains pretty quickly after we cross into Maryland, so we better not wait too long to get fuel," Ben added.

"How much longer will we be on the interstate?" Allie asked.

"This will pretty much take us all the way to Baltimore, but we'll get off outside the city onto 695 and go around. It's the fastest way up north and around the bay. I think it'll keep us far enough outside the city that we won't have any problems," Ben said without looking up from the map.

Joel put the Blazer in gear and accelerated out from under the cool shade of the overpass. He felt the heat of the sun immediately, and even with his sunglasses on, he was forced to squint until his eyes adjusted to the glare.

Sandy sighed. "Wow, I forgot how hot it was."

"It's a little after noon, so this is the worst of it. It should start to cool down in a couple hours. Not that it's much of a consolation right now." Ben shrugged.

Joel looked down at the radio as it continued to search through the channels. They hadn't heard a thing since the emergency broadcast. Not so much as a crackle of static had come over the speakers.

"Where do you think the radio signal came from?" Sandy asked.

"Not sure. Maybe D.C. or the Pentagon? We're getting close to a lot of government facilities, and Camp David isn't too far from here, either," Ben answered.

Allie joined the conversation. "But why do you think it cut out?"

"My guess is they're in the beginning stages of reestablishing communications and trying to get the power grid back up. It might still be some time before they manage that. From what we've seen, the electrical damage done by the EMPs was pretty extensive. It's not like working the bugs out of a program. There's actual physical damage that will need to be repaired. Anything that was running at the time of the attack would have experienced a massive power surge, probably like getting hit by lightning but on a much larger scale and a lot more powerful."

Joel slowed down to swerve around a burned-out delivery truck that had become entangled in the guardrail. The guardrail had done its job and kept the truck from going over the edge and into the ravine below, but it hadn't mattered.

The truck itself had burned down to nothing but the frame. Whatever it was hauling had melted and hung from the steel skeleton of the trailer all the way down to the road. The fire had long gone out, and the material re-solidified, forming a dull black coating that would hold the truck in its place indefinitely.

It was an odd sight, and enough so that the conversation in the truck paused as they all took it in. The wrecked truck jackknifed when it had hit the guardrail and the trailer was blocking most of the highway. With a guardrail on the other side as well, it only left Joel with part of a lane and the shoulder to get by.

They were barely moving now as he picked his way around the debris and prepared to drive around the truck. They were close enough for his dad to reach out and touch it if he had wanted to. The pungent odor of burnt plastic filled the Blazer and remained with them even as they pulled away.

"Oh, that's strong." Allie winced as she covered her mouth and nose with her hand.

Joel accelerated as quickly as he could to get away from the smell and fought the urge to look at the cab of the delivery truck when they passed. He knew well enough what he would see if he did.

In the past week and a half, he'd seen enough bodies to supply a lifetime's worth of bad dreams. It was bad enough that they were all decomposing and what little skin remained was beginning to look like leather.

But the worst thing about the bodies was the horrific poses most of them were stuck in. Joel couldn't seem to get them out of his head. It was like someone had stuck them in the worst positions possible for the most dramatic effect.

In the last few days, he had tried his best to not to look at the bodies when they passed by. He was finding it easier as the days passed to ignore the wrecks altogether, and he wondered if that was a good thing or not.

· 32 ·

"Welcome to Maryland." Ben read the sign out loud as they left West Virginia behind. There were times in the last week or so that he thought they might never see that sign. And although they still had a long drive in front of them, he couldn't help but feel a little joy over the accomplishment.

"How are we looking on gas?" Ben asked.

"Just over a quarter tank," Joel reported.

The rolling hills were slowly building into mountains, and although they were small in comparison to the Rockies, the elevation changes were working the Blazer hard. They would need to stop and get fuel before they got any deeper into the Appalachians.

Several miles passed before Allie spotted a small gas station down off the highway in a valley ahead. Joel followed the exit ramp and pulled into the parking area of the store. The small gas station was partially burned down and one of the gas pumps out front was ripped from its base and left lying in the middle of the parking lot.

Ben cautiously surveyed the area as Joel made the standard drive around what was left of the building.

"Looks good to me," Joel said.

"Yeah, let's try to make it a quick one and get back on the road." Ben wasn't crazy about the fact that there were several other buildings nearby and didn't want to stop here any longer than necessary. He couldn't put his finger on it, but something didn't feel right to him.

He felt like they were being watched but resolved to chalk it up to nerves. He didn't want to let his guard down now. They'd come a long way and been through a lot, but they weren't there yet. They still needed to remain vigilant.

Joel parked the truck and everyone unloaded quickly. Gunner did his usual and headed off to explore the perimeter of the parking lot, following his nose wherever it led him. Ben and Joel didn't waste any time and got set up to pump gas immediately while the girls headed off to find a little privacy.

"Don't go too far, and be careful." Ben didn't want to sound overprotective, but he didn't want any trouble today, either.

"We won't be gone long." Allie rested her shotgun over her shoulder as the two headed off toward the burned-out building.

Ben was glad to see she had the shotgun with her. At some point in time, he'd have to give Sandy a crash-course on the guns and give her something to carry. Maybe he could do it when they got to Jack's. He didn't want to take any time away from driving today. He hadn't been sure yesterday if they would be able to finish the drive today, but now that they were here, the reality of doing just that sunk in.

Ben had seen the sign for the Savage River State Forest back a few miles and he remembered Casey's dad talking about coming up here on several occasions to go fly-fishing. It was the only place in Maryland with decent trout water he used to say. Ben also remembered Jack saying it was a five-hour drive, give or take, from his house in Berlin, Maryland.

Of course, that was using a more direct route over the Chesapeake Bay Bridge and traveling at normal highway speed, neither of which they could do. But even with their alternative route and slower speed, he knew it was possible to reach Jack's house tonight.

His plan was to check for the kids at Jack's first. They would pass by his place on the way to his ex's place anyway. And he had a feeling they would all be there—at least he hoped they would be.

Jack was getting on in years and he had some health issues, but Ben knew for a fact that he kept extra supplies and food on hand in the outbuilding behind his house. He also had an old Jeep Scrambler that he used for hunting. He wasn't sure if he still had the Jeep or the supplies, but either way, Jack was Casey's and the kids' best chance for survival.

His ex had rented a condo in Ocean City when she moved away with the kids and lived about 15 minutes from Jack's place, over a couple bridges that crossed a small bay. Ben doubted they would stay in Ocean City after the attacks, and if they didn't go to Jack's on their own, he would probably come and get them.

"I can take over if you want." Joel was carrying the empty cans and set them down near the pump.

Ben pulled the nozzle out of the truck and handed it to Joel. "Sure, just fill the cans. The truck is full."

As Ben screwed the gas cap back on he was startled by a high-pitched scream from behind the gas station. Instinctively, he reached back and drew his pistol.

"Stay here and get those tanks filled and strapped to the truck!" Ben barked as he started for the building. He ran around the front of the truck and was disappointed to see Gunner in the front corner of the parking lot. Ben had hoped that he was with the girls.

Gunner immediately stopped what he was doing when he saw Ben running and chased after him.

BOOM!

The unmistakable report of Allie's 20-gauge echoed off the surrounding buildings. Ben and Gunner rounded the corner of the burned-out gas station and almost ran into the girls. Allie was still holding the shotgun out in front of her and trembling. Sandy was next to her with a hand on Allie's shoulder. Their faces were pale white, and neither one bothered to look at him or Gunner.

"What happened?" Ben breathed heavily.

"Snake! Big snake!" Allie looked like she wanted to say more but couldn't get it out at the moment. She pointed to the ground a few yards away instead. There, in front of the girls, was the largest copperhead snake Ben had ever seen. There weren't any copperheads in Colorado, but he had seen his fair share of them while training at Fort Benning in Georgia.

"It came out of the grass and chased us." Allie's voice trembled.

"I didn't know snakes did that," Sandy said.

Ben quickly backpedaled to the corner of the building and made eye contact with Joel, who was frantically cranking the fuel pump handle.

"It's okay, Joel. Just a snake." Ben rejoined Allie and her mom. Gunner was eyeing the snake as it writhed and twisted itself into knots on the ground. Allie had blown the head clean off, but the snake continued moving through nervous twitches.

"Gunner, no." Ben held the dog away with a stern voice.

"Is it still alive?" Allie asked.

"No, just nerves." Ben took a closer look as Joel came around the corner of the building.

"Whoa! That's huge! What is it?" he asked.

"It's a copperhead, and yes, they are venomous," Ben answered.

"Are you guys okay?" Joel looked at Allie and her mom.

"Yeah, just scared us. That's all. It wouldn't stop coming at us. I had to shoot it." Allie exhaled.

Ben was now relieved that Gunner hadn't been with them. The dog would have surely tried to intervene and gotten himself bitten in the process.

"Well, I've had enough excitement. I'm ready to get back in the truck and get out of here," Allie declared.

That suited Ben just fine. He was glad she had used the gun and defended herself, but he was concerned about the gunshot drawing attention to them.

They all made their way back to the truck, and Ben helped Joel get the fuel cans strapped down while the girls and Gunner loaded up.

Ben kept a nervous eye on the surrounding buildings and houses. He thought he saw someone looking through a curtain from a house across the street but wasn't sure.

"I'll drive," Ben said.

"Okay, I can drive more later on if you need me to." Joel pulled the strap tight and headed for the passenger's side of the truck.

Ben got into the driver's seat and started the engine. He was disappointed that he didn't feel more comfortable here. It would have been nice to eat something while they were stopped, but he couldn't shake the uneasy feeling this place gave him. They'd find somewhere better down the road, somewhere more isolated.

They had come too far to take chances now.

· 33 ·

Once back out on the highway, Allie and her mother regained their composure from their encounter with the snake.

"That was good shooting back there, Allie. Good job," Ben said.

"Thanks, I've never killed anything before." Allie shrugged.

"I'm not sure what was more surprising: the snake or the way you handled that gun," Sandy said.

"Allie's a pretty good shot, as it turns out." Joel twisted around in his seat and smiled.

Sandy cleared her throat. "Well, I have a little confession to make, Allie. I've been taking a class and learning how to shoot, back in Durango. I wasn't sure how you'd feel about having a gun in the house. But I thought it would be a good idea with us living alone."

"I would have been okay with that, Mom." Allie pulled out the .38 and showed it to her mother.

Sandy laughed. "I can see that now."

"Here, Mom. Take it. I mean, if that's okay with you." Allie shifted her gaze to Ben.

"Yeah, it's good with me. I think it's a good idea. I was actually thinking about that earlier."

Allie handed the gun to her mom. "I like the shotgun better anyway."

Sandy looked it over. "Thanks, it's a lot like the one I was learning with."

Ben felt better knowing that he wasn't going to have to teach Sandy how to use a weapon, and what's more, she had taken a class on shooting. One less thing to worry about, and the way things were going, it would be an asset to have another gun ready to offer backup, should the need arise.

Ben was pleased to see the interstate remained mostly clear, especially now that their visibility was limited by the turns and elevation changes as the road followed the easiest route through the mountains.

Allie handed out Clif Bars and apples while Ben continued to drive. They all seemed satisfied to make that their lunch and unanimously decided to forgo pulling over somewhere to fix a proper meal.

After an hour or so of driving, it was obvious to Ben that they would be stopping again for gas sooner than he wanted to admit. The constant elevation change of the road was causing them to burn through their fuel at a staggering rate. The added weight of an extra person and supplies they'd taken in made a difference as well.

He could feel it in the way the Blazer responded when he maneuvered around the wrecks. It was sluggish compared to when it had just been the three of them and Gunner. It had also been balanced a little better then and hadn't had a giant duffel bag strapped to the roof.

All this only served as a reminder that they would have to make some major changes for the return trip. He still wasn't sure if a camper or a second vehicle was the way to go. They were probably going to have to settle for whatever they could find.

He resolved to make that the number one priority when they got to Jack's. At the very least, they would be adding Bradley and Emma to their crew. He wasn't sure what would happen with his ex-wife, and frankly, she could do what she wanted as far as he was concerned. But he wasn't leaving Maryland without the kids.

He had no idea what they would find when they got there. He tried to force the negative thoughts from his mind, but he couldn't help but think about the possibility that they would be too late or that he wouldn't be able to find the kids at all.

What if Casey and the kids had gone somewhere with her boyfriend?

Ben tried to clear his head and focus on the here

and now. He watched the landscape pass by and thought about how some sections of the road, where it cut through the rock, reminded him of home, a place that seemed impossibly far away right now. Durango, he knew, was more than just across the country and thousands of miles behind them.

It felt much more distant than that, like something he would never see again—at least not the way he remembered it before the bombs.

· 34 ·

The miles rolled by, and other than a few comments about the scenery, the truck was quiet. Maybe because for the first time in a while they were offered a view thanks to the elevation of the mountains.

As they crossed over the highest point and headed down the eastern slope of the Appalachians, they could see for several miles in almost every direction.

The thing Ben noticed most was the color of the trees. He hadn't really paid attention to the coloring so much before and just thought that everything looked a little dry. But now that he could see large swaths of forest, it was obvious that the dry weather and environmental conditions were taking their toll on the vegetation.

It was nearly the end of June, but the colors of the trees more closely resembled that of fall. He also noticed patches of forest that had lost their foliage altogether and he wondered if they were dying from a lack of water or if there was something more sinister at work.

Ben checked the fuel gauge, and although they had a little less than half a tank, he wanted to stop soon and top it off. They had enough gas to make it to Baltimore but not enough to get much farther than that, and he wanted to fuel up before they got too close to the city.

By the time they had reached Fredrick, Maryland, the needle on the fuel gauge had fallen close to the quarter-tank mark and it was time to find somewhere to stop. With the mountains behind them and a little luck, the next tank should carry them the rest of the way.

They managed to find an isolated gas station just outside of Mount Airy, Maryland, and pulled over. Everyone got out of the truck to stretch their legs but stayed close.

Even Gunner seemed reluctant to wander too far from the Blazer, and after a quick walk around to mark a few spots, he jumped into the truck on his own and waited patiently there for the rest of them.

Ben and Joel made quick work of pumping gas and they were loaded up and back on the road in no time. Everyone seemed to be equally motivated to keep things moving along now that they were closing in on their destination.

Sandy was feeling a little car sick and swapped places with Joel in the passenger's seat.

The activity excited Gunner and he wagged his tail wildly, thumping the rear window like a drum. He was clearly pleased to have both Joel and Allie in the back, close to him, and he hung his big head over the back of the rear seat between them and panted loudly.

"How far do you think we are now, Dad?"

"We're probably about an hour from Baltimore. After that, maybe four hours, depending on the roads." Ben adjusted the side vent window to force more air into the truck.

The temperature was quickly climbing as the sun beat down through the yellowish haze in the air. The air had cleared a little and seemed almost normal when they passed over the mountains, but now that they were dropping in elevation, it thickened again and returned to the haziness that they had almost grown used to.

It felt thicker this time, though, and Ben wondered if it was due to their proximity to D.C. or Baltimore.

The landscape changed quickly from rolling hills and sprawling farms to apartment buildings and big-box stores. Sandy pointed out a sign for the 695 expressway around Baltimore, and not long after that, Ben saw the exit. He accelerated toward the ramp, but a large accident quickly stopped their progress.

A delivery truck had collided with several other vehicles and blocked the exit ramp between the guardrails.

He was forced to do a three-point turn and head back to the interstate. He drove down to the westbound exit and they made their way onto the expressway from the other direction. They were closing in on the city, and the roads were starting to show it as abandoned cars and accidents became more frequent.

Ben was encouraged, though, in spite of the more congested road. They had finally made it to the end of I-70. The road they had traveled on since Kansas was finally behind them, and although they still had a long day ahead, Ben felt like they had passed a milestone in their journey.

Many times in the past several days he had doubted whether they would ever get this far. But they had, and now it was just a matter of less than a couple hundred miles to Emma and Bradley.

It should have given him some sense of relief or at least satisfaction, but it didn't. Instead, he was even more apprehensive. The fact that he knew what kind of city Baltimore was didn't help.

Hopefully, they could get around the city without any incidents. He thought about what a shame it was that they couldn't use the Chesapeake Bay Bridge. It would shave a couple hours off the trip, but they had come too far to take chances and he quickly dismissed the thought.

Going around the bridge was the right thing to do, and as tempting as it was to try the shorter route, he was going to have to trust his gut on this and leave it at that.

As they made their way around the expressway, it was obvious that Baltimore had suffered catastrophic losses. They were too far outside the city to see any details, but the large plumes of dark smoke still rising over what had been Baltimore was a telltale sign of the destruction. It reminded Ben of the scene outside St. Louis.

He wondered if Baltimore was one of the locations that had been hit. The emergency broadcast they picked up on the radio said 23 detonations, but they lost the signal before they were named. It would have been nice to know where they had hit.

They'd seen a few of the places firsthand and the major had told them about a couple, but there was no telling where the other bombs had gone off.

There were definitely areas they would be sure to avoid on the return trip, but for all they knew, they could just as easily end up somewhere worse off than what they were trying to avoid. They had tried several times since the broadcast to pick up the signal again, but they hadn't heard a thing.

The expressway was a mess. Cars and trucks were scattered about like Matchbox cars left behind by a messy child. The only saving grace was the width of the road.

In most places, it was six lanes wide on each side, allowing room to navigate around the obstacles. There was no getting around the death and destruction, though.

And even though they had seen their fair share of wrecks and bodies, nothing compared to the carnage laid out before them on the expressway. There seemed to be an endless supply of corpses posed in every gruesome position imaginable.

Silence fell over the truck as they passed through the area at an unfortunately slow rate of speed, forcing them all to take in the spectacle. It was impossible to ignore the scene, and it didn't matter which direction they looked: now there was death everywhere.

The bodies that hadn't been reduced to charcoaled remains showed signs of being picked at by animals. The off-white of exposed bones reflected the bright sun through large holes of leathery skin.

Ben went as fast as he could, but there were so many wrecks to drive around that it was impossible to maintain a decent speed. This was going to add some time to their already lengthened route to the kids.

He was relieved to see the congested expressway start to open up as they approached the exit for I-95 north. He steered the Blazer around a pile of mangled cars and took the exit, leaving the expressway behind.

The interstate was heavily littered with wrecks as well, but it was nowhere near as crowded as the expressway had been. The road here was also four lanes wide but had large paved shoulders with a wide strip of grass on either side. This made it easy to get around what obstacles there were and also allowed him to pick up some much-needed speed.

They followed 95 north for about an hour before crossing into northern Delaware and making a right toward the eastern shore of Maryland.

They were less than a couple hours away at this point, and if he could maintain this speed, they would be there before dark.

· 35 ·

What should have only taken them a couple of hours under normal circumstances took closer to three and a half. And as they made their final turn onto the road that led to Grandpa Jack's, the sun was low on the horizon.

The anticipation was almost too much to bear, and the last few miles of road seemed to go on forever.

Even Gunner was unsettled and was somehow aware that they were nearing something of importance. Ben watched the dog in the rearview mirror as he shifted restlessly from one position to the other, occasionally letting out a nervous whine.

"Easy, boy." Allie stroked Gunner's head.

"He knows we're almost there," Joel said.

"Yes, we are." Ben recognized the black mailbox with a mallard duck painted on the side.

It marked the entrance of the long gravel lane that led back to Jack's. The old farmhouse sat back off the road several hundred yards and was surrounded by 20 acres of open flat fields and a few old chicken houses. Jack leased the land out to a local farmer who rotated his crops from soybeans to corn every other year.

Jack preferred when the farmer grew corn, as it helped block the house from the road. Ben remembered when he and Casey had come out for a visit last time. The corn was taller than their rental car and the house wasn't visible from the road at all.

But that wasn't the case now, and they could clearly see the house over the dead rows of small soybean plants. From the looks of things, they hadn't seen any rain around here in a while, either.

The house was just as Ben remembered it, except for its poor condition on the exterior. It was a small two-story Victorian-style farmhouse with painted yellow wooden siding that always seemed to be peeling in one spot or another, but now the whole house looked like it could use attention.

Jack had refused to pay someone to paint the house in spite of Ben and Casey trying to convince him otherwise. He argued that there was no need to pay someone to do something he could do himself. Jack was a stubborn old guy and usually managed to keep up with it.

But now in his old age, he had apparently fallen behind with the exterior maintenance. The house looked much older than Ben recalled, and it gave him cause for concern.

Maybe things had gotten worse with his health in recent months. Ben was suddenly more worried than he had been during the entire trip. What if there was no one here? He took a deep breath and tried to calm himself. *They're here. They have to be.*

"Are we here?" Allie leaned forward and looked out the front window as Ben steered the Blazer onto the gravel road that led up to Jack's house.

"This is it!" Ben nodded, but he had a hard time believing it himself.

"The house looks really run down. I don't remember it looking like this." Joel joined Allie as he leaned forward to get a better look.

"It doesn't look like anybody lives here," Sandy added.

She was right. There was no car in the driveway and the place felt abandoned.

"He parks everything in the outbuilding usually." Ben motioned toward a large metal outbuilding behind the house. He knew Jack kept his boat in there, as well as the old Jeep he used for hunting.

It was a large building and there was plenty of room in there for the Ford pickup he drove on a regular basis as well. Besides, knowing Jack, he was sure he would have moved everything out of sight when things got bad.

The gravel crunched and popped under the tires

as the Blazer came to a stop in front of the brick walkway that led to the front door. Ben turned the truck off and looked back at Joel.

"Listen. Hear that?" Ben heard a dog barking inside the house.

"Is that Sam?" Joel asked. "Sam is my grandpa's dog," he added.

Ben nodded. It was definitely Sam, Jack's yellow Lab and long-time hunting partner. Jack and Sam went everywhere together, and there was no way he would leave Sam behind if they had gone somewhere.

Ben got out of the truck and was followed by Gunner, who had pushed his way between Joel and Allie impatiently. The dog hit the ground and bounded straight up the walkway toward the house, sniffing the ground loudly as he went. Joel climbed out after his dad, and Allie got out behind her mother on the passenger's side.

"Oh my, what is that?" Allie winced as the smell of death wafted over them on a warm breeze. Fortunately, the wind shifted directions and the intensity of the smell diminished substantially.

"Dead chickens. We passed a lot of commercial chicken houses on the way in," Ben answered.

More than a few of the surrounding farms were home to row after row of the long red buildings used for raising chickens. Each house held thousands of birds, and without power to keep the cooling fans running and the feeders working, they would have all died days ago.

Ben thought back to a few phone conversations he'd had with Jack when he had mentioned that "the smell is the price I pay for living in the country." Jack said it was always the worst during the hot months of summer, when the mortality rate of the chickens was high.

But Ben wasn't concerned about chickens or the smell right now, and his heart began to race as he approached the front door.

"Jack? Hello?" Ben called out as he peered cautiously through the small half-round window in the top of the door. He followed it up with a few quick knocks and then stepped to the side.

Jack was liable to have a gun at the ready for any unwanted visitors, and Ben didn't want to risk being shot. Sam erupted into another volley of barks, and as Ben peeked in the window again, he could see the large yellow Lab standing guard in the foyer. Gunner answered with a couple sharp barks of his own and whined at Ben nervously.

Ben pulled away from the window again and turned to see Joel coming up the steps to join him on the porch.

"See anybody?" Joel asked.

"Just Sam in there going crazy. They have to be around somewhere. Jack doesn't go anywhere without that dog."

Ben leapt down the three brick steps and backpedaled away from the covered porch so he could see the second floor of the house.

"Hello? Jack, it's me, Ben. Is anybody in there?" He cupped his hands around his mouth in an effort to direct his voice toward the large window that led to the master bedroom.

"Somebody's in there! I just saw a curtain move over there!" Allie pointed to a second-floor window at the corner of the house.

Ben looked but was too late to see anything. As he scanned the other windows for any signs of life, Sam suddenly stopped barking and it was very quiet.

What if it wasn't Jack and Casey or the kids? What if someone had broken in and was living there? Sam had a mean bark, but Ben knew the dog was a big pushover and, unlike Gunner, would cozy up to anyone that would scratch him.

He cleared his T-shirt away from the holstered pistol and prepared for the worst.

· 36 ·

"I hear somebody moving around inside," Joel reported from the porch.

"Get away from the door," Ben ordered.

Joel stepped to the side and backed away as the front door creaked open. Ben felt his muscles tense up as he moved his hand closer to the pistol, but he quickly stopped when he saw a weak and frail-looking Jack stagger out onto the porch.

"Grandpa!" Joel exclaimed.

"Joel, Ben... I don't believe it!" Jack set the shotgun he was carrying butt-end down and leaned it against the doorframe.

"Well, get over here!" Jack reached out to Joel and pulled him in for a hug. Ben felt immediate relief at the sight of Jack and took a few long strides to get back up on the porch quickly.

"Hey there, old man!" Jack reached out to shake Ben's hand while he continued to use Joel for support.

Ben hated to admit it, but Jack looked really old, a lot older than he should have. The fact that he'd also lost a lot of weight since they'd last seen him didn't help any.

"It's good to see you, Jack!" Ben took his hand and felt the frailness of his grip, a big change from the hardy handshakes he'd come to expect from the man over the years.

Jack shifted his weight onto Ben now as he stepped away from Joel and looked him over.

"My goodness, I barely recognize you, Joel! You look like a full-grown man." Jack chuckled.

Joel blushed at the comment and looked down at the ground just as Sam forced the door open and sauntered out onto the porch. The two dogs took cautious positions with tails in the air as they met for the first time and proceeded to sniff each other from head to tail. Sam turned her attention to Ben and Joel briefly to receive a few scratches before resuming her inspection of Gunner.

Allie and her mother made their way up onto the porch, pausing briefly to make way for the dogs, who had begun a playful game of chase down the steps and out into the yard. Ben would make introductions soon enough, but right now, he had to have an answer to the question that had been on his mind for the last 2000 miles.

"Are the kids okay?"

But before Jack could answer the question,

Bradley and Emma appeared in the doorway behind him.

"Dad," they cried in unison.

Ben dropped to his knees and caught both of them as they ran into his arms. Joel joined in and wrapped his arms around his brother and sister from the back. The four of them remained locked together for a few moments before Ben pulled back to get a good look at his two youngest children.

He was pleasantly surprised to see they looked remarkably healthy and happy. Other than the fact that he was sure they had grown since he last saw them in person over Christmas break, they looked the same. He wasn't sure what he expected, but certainly not this. With the kids still hanging on to him, Ben looked up at Jack.

"Casey?"

Jack's smile faded and he looked away for a moment before making eye contact with Ben again.

"I don't know." Jack shook his head.

"What do you mean? Where's Mom?" Joel pulled away from the group hug and stood up to face Jack.

"I mean I don't know. I'm sorry." Jack shifted his gaze to Ben. "She was away on a cruise with the boyfriend. Brad and Emma were staying with me while they were out of town. Dan had some type of convention to go to in Orlando, and then they were doing a cruise out of Cape Canaveral when it was over. They were supposed to come back the Sunday after it happened. They must have still been on the boat when…" Jack stopped when he looked down and noticed Bradley and Emma listening.

Joel's eyes were red and beginning to tear up.

"So she's probably stuck on a boat somewhere?" Joel cleared his throat and swallowed hard as he fought to maintain a steady tone.

Ben looked at Joel and then at the younger two. "It's better than being stuck at an airport or, worse yet, in mid-flight. It means there's a good chance she's alive. Your mom is smart and she's tougher than you think."

Bradley spoke up. "You really think Mom is okay?"

"Yeah, buddy, I do." Ben tried to sound confident and hugged them both again.

"That's what I told them. Casey can handle herself," Jack added.

Ben, anxious to change the topic for the kids' sake, stood up and introduced Allie and her mother to Jack and the kids.

"I've heard a lot about you guys. It's nice to finally meet you." Allie stooped down to greet the kids.

Bradley was shy and didn't respond with anything more than a nod as he remained attached to Ben, but Emma reached out to shake her hand.

"Hi," Emma said quietly.

Their handshake was interrupted by Sam, who joined everyone up on the porch, with Gunner right behind her. The dogs were covered in dust and dry grass from their escapades in the yard. Sam forced her snoot into Allie's still-outstretched hand, and Emma smiled.

"I see you're a jealous dog, too." Allie looked at Emma and smiled before giving Sam a few good rubs on the head and the attention she demanded.

"Why don't you guys grab your stuff and bring it in? I was about to make dinner." Jack opened the door and was about to go in when the two dirty and panting dogs pushed past everyone and made their way in first.

"You should probably park out back by the garage. Just to be safe. I haven't had any trouble, but a few of my neighbors have. I've been keeping everything inside since it happened." Jack made eye contact with Ben in a way that made him think there was more to that story, but he didn't want to get into it with the kids there.

Ben nodded. "Sounds good."

They all walked out to the truck together to get their bags while Jack headed into the house ahead of them to get dinner started. Bradley and Emma stayed close to Ben and Joel and helped carry the gear inside. Ben set his bag down a couple feet inside the door and started back to the truck so he could pull it around to the outbuilding, but Bradley stopped him as he wrapped his arms around Ben's waist.

"I knew you would come for us." Bradley's voice was muffled as he buried his face in his dad's side.

Ben smiled and hugged him back. "It's okay, buddy. We're all here now."

Bradley eventually released his father and wiped away a few tears as he stepped back.

Joel came over and put his hand on his brother's shoulder. "It'll be okay."

Jack cleared his throat from across the room. "Why don't you guys take Allie and her mom upstairs and let them get cleaned up? I'm sure you're all tired. I have a couple spare rooms upstairs. Sandy, you and Allie can have one. Joel, you and your dad can share the other one. I was going to run the generator to make dinner, so you might as well make good use of it and get a shower if you want one."

"Thank you. That would be wonderful." Sandy's eyes widened with excitement.

"No problem! Ben, I'll meet you out back with the truck and we'll see if we can't make room for it inside the garage." Jack headed for the back door out through the kitchen.

By the time Ben drove the Blazer around to the back side of the house, Jack had the large overhead garage door open and was hooking the tractor to the trailer hitch on the Jon boat. Ben was glad to see the old Jeep Scrambler that Jack used for hunting parked alongside the boat.

Ben put the Blazer into park and hurried over to help him get the boat hitched. Jack pulled the camouflaged duck boat out into the yard and parked it behind a couple trees off to the side of the property before driving the tractor back over to the outbuilding.

Ben already had the Blazer backed in where the boat had been and closed the large garage door behind Jack while he returned the tractor to its spot inside the building.

Looking around the garage, he could see not much had changed from the last time he'd been here. The shelves were still crowded with tools, boxes, and a bunch of other unidentifiable things stuffed in between—except around the Blazer, where the boat had been parked.

That area of shelving was filled with an assortment of duck decoys and hunting equipment. Over on the end, near a climbing tree stand Jack used for deer hunting, were a few large boxes marked MEAL, READY TO EAT/INDIVIDUAL. He was glad to see that Jack still had the MREs on hand, but he noticed Jack's pickup was nowhere to be seen.

Ben watched as Jack stiffly climbed down off the tractor and headed his way. When had he gotten so old? It had been a few years since he'd seen Jack, but he wasn't prepared to find him in this condition. He knew the man had been having some health issues but had no idea it had taken its toll on him in such a drastic way.

Ben couldn't help but feel a little angry at his ex-wife for leaving the kids with Jack. Not a smart move, even under good circumstances, in his opinion. There was no point in wasting time thinking about that now, though. Thankfully, the kids were healthy and seemed to be in good spirits, all things considered.

He would never admit it to the kids, but the chances of Casey making it through this were slim to none.

If they were on a cruise ship, there was no telling what would become of them. The ship's systems would have all suffered catastrophic failures. They'd be stranded and adrift on the ocean, trapped with hundreds—no, maybe a couple thousand— strangers all fighting over dwindling resources. It wouldn't be pretty; that was for sure.

As Ben began to run through the possible scenarios in his mind, Jack fired up the generator.

· 37 ·

Jack motioned for Ben to follow him outside and away from the noise of the generator. He led him through a smaller door in the side of the garage and locked it behind Ben before continuing on to the house.

"Can't be too careful. People are starting to reach out farther and farther from town in search of food and water. Friends of mine that live a few miles closer in told me some people came around their place and made threats. He and his wife stopped by a couple days ago on their way out of town. They have some family in North Carolina they were going to try to get to. They offered to take us with them, but I had a feeling you'd be coming to get the kids. Besides, I've lived here my whole life. I'm not about to go anywhere." Jack stopped walking when he reached a small garden halfway between the house and the outbuilding.

He pulled a pocket knife out and flicked it open

before bending down with a grunt. He separated a few zucchini and yellow squash from a tangle of vines on the ground with a surprising amount of agility compared to the other tasks Ben had watched him struggle with since they'd arrived. The old man still had a little life left in him after all.

Jack pointed to a bucket that was hanging near a hand pump at the far end of the garden.

"Fill that up, would you? The water isn't great, but it's not bad after you boil it, and it's the only reason these vegetables are growing."

"We haven't seen much rain since Colorado," Ben said.

"Haven't seen any here," Jack quickly added.

"So I assume your plan is to take the kids back to Colorado?" Jack stood up, slowly juggling the fresh-cut vegetables and catching Ben off guard with his direct question.

"Yeah, that's the plan. It's the only place I'm confident I can provide for everyone on a sustainable basis." Ben gave the pump handle a few cranks before the water started to trickle out. It wasn't until it began to accumulate in the bottom of the bucket that he saw it had a brownish tint to it.

Jack exhaled loudly as he folded the knife and tucked it away in his pocket. He looked past Ben, out toward the horizon. "How bad is it out there?"

"It's not good. You wouldn't believe some of the

things we've seen and been through trying to get here."

"I can imagine." Jack shook his head and started to make his way back to the house again.

"Colorado is the only place I know I can take care of the kids." Ben paused for a second. He probably knew the answer to what he was about to suggest but decided to make the offer anyway. "I want you to come with us, Jack."

The old man stopped shuffling forward and turned around, looking out over the yard as he did.

"You see that magnolia tree over there? My wife and I planted it shortly after Casey was born." He cleared his throat before continuing. "Carol's ashes are spread around that tree." Jack sighed.

Ben remembered flying out for the funeral when Casey's mom passed away several years ago. It was about the same time they started having problems with the marriage.

"No, this is home. Anyway, someone's got to be here if Casey makes it back," Jack said with a finality that made it clear he wasn't leaving.

Ben knew the possibilities of Casey ever returning were slim, but he didn't have the heart to try to use that point to convince Jack to come with them. He already felt guilty enough taking the kids away and leaving him here all alone. It was useless to try to convince the old man otherwise, and he knew it.

Ben also knew that the best chance of survival for all of them was in Durango. He and Joel could provide food and clean water on a consistent basis back home with little effort.

"You're not all going to fit in the Blazer, are you?" Jack asked.

"No, I don't think so. We're going to have to figure something out."

"You'll take the Jeep. I won't take no for an answer." Jack nodded toward the outbuilding.

"But what about you? I didn't see your pickup anywhere. What if you need to go somewhere?"

"Me? Where do I need to go? The Smiths down the road are there if I need something. I wrecked the pickup a while back and didn't bother replacing it. Casey wanted me to stop driving altogether and even got a service to come out twice a week to clean the house and check in on me. Can you believe that?" He rolled his eyes at Ben.

"You think the Jeep will make the trip?" From what he remembered, the Scrambler was pretty rough, and Jack only used it for hunting.

"I had it fixed up when I lost the pickup. It's been my daily driver for a while now. Of course, Casey doesn't know that." Jack smiled as he made his way up to the rear deck and set the produce down by the grill.

Ben noticed a new, full soft top on the Jeep when he was in the garage but didn't give it much thought. The Jeep was small, but it would work just fine and could easily haul two people, a dog, and some gear. It would also burn less gas than a bigger truck and a lot less gas than the Blazer would burn if it was pulling a camper.

Ben joined him on the deck and set the metal bucket down on the side burner as Jack lit the pilot light on the gas-fired grill. The little circle erupted with a whoosh of flames as they curled around the bottom of the bucket. The two men stepped back from the grill and watched.

"I can't thank you enough, Jack, for taking care of the kids and offering the Jeep." Ben reached out to shake his hand.

Jack surprised him with a firm grip this time as he looked him in the eye.

"You can thank me by resting here a couple days and then getting those kids back to Colorado safe and sound."

Ben nodded. "That's my plan."

And if they had made it here, they could make it home.

Find out about Bruno Miller's next book by signing up for his newsletter:
http://brunomillerauthor.com/sign-up/

No spam, no junk, just news (sales, freebies, and releases). Scouts honor.

Enjoy the book?
Help the series grow by telling a friend about it
and taking the time to leave a review.

About the Author

BRUNO MILLER is the author of the Dark Road series. He's a military vet who likes to spend his downtime hanging out with his wife and kids, or getting in some range time. He believes in being prepared for any situation.

http://brunomillerauthor.com/

https://www.facebook.com/BrunoMillerAuthor/

Made in United States
Troutdale, OR
01/22/2024

17061346R00146